PARASOMNIA

K.J. BECK

ANOMALY
press

This is a work of fiction. Names, characters, places, and events either are the product of the author's imagination or are used fictitiously, and any resemblance to actual persons, living or dead, events, or locales is entirely coincidental.

PARASOMNIA

Cover art by Fendie Daywalker
@Fendiedaywalker on Instagram

Cover design by K. J. Beck

ISBN: 978-1-7369909-0-2

Library of Congress Control Number: 2021936347

Published by Anomaly Press
Washington, D. C.

Anomaly Press, LLC
P.O. Box 562
Amissville, VA 20106

Anomaly Press online:
http://www.anomaly.press

Printed in the United States of America

To my beautiful wife Natalie,
Without whom none of this would be possible.

CONTENTS

INTRODUCTION

There was a path, some series of unalterable events and circumstances that led you to this moment where you now find yourself reading these words. You may wonder, what is this thing that I now hold in my hand? On its face, this is a science fiction novel, however, that classification was merely an unintended consequence of an overactive imagination. In writing this novel, I set out to put to paper something that burned within me to escape. The story itself started as a dream, a single floating telephone, yellowed and outdated, hanging in the void of a perfect darkness. I started this book with no plot, no outline, no ending, no goal in mind. There was nothing but a spark, and I fanned it until it became a flame.

INTRODUCTION

This work comes from my personal darkness, from places deep inside of me I had believed long-since discarded. As I wrote this book, I peeled away my flesh and dug deep into my soul to pull out that darkness, to lay it before me, to bring it into the light and examine it in all its hideous beauty.

You will not find a good and likable person in these characters, but I do not intend them to be likable. My intent is for you to see yourself, your flaws, your demons, your own personal darkness in the mirror of these people, these amalgams of my past, these specters of a life long-forgotten.

Never have I been prouder of something I created and never have I hated anything more. Each day I resist the urge to incinerate it, to delete the files, and wipe it from existence. There are those who will read this book and enjoy an interesting and mind-bending plot. There will be others who find more within these pages than they expected. I do not claim brilliance, for such a claim would be baseless and vain. No, this book doesn't belong to me, it belongs to the universe, and to you, and it is yours to make of it what you will.

This book exists as the result of terrible things, and years wasted. Darkness made this book possible, the darkness of wasted youth, of reckless abandon, of hopeless addictions. There are many people for whom I would like to credit with making this book a reality. Some of them are no longer with us, others I have not spoken to in decades, yet without them this work would not exist. I will not name them, in part because to credit them would be to thank them for helping destroy me, and also because the dead should enjoy their slumber. However, I thank them all for the heart-break and the sorrow, the pain and the misery, the darkness and the suffering. We shared some experiences that will remain in darkness and silence forever, and others that now live as metaphors inside these pages.

There are those whom I would like to name, those who supported me on this journey, who gave me feedback and critique, who spoke kind words when I wanted to give up. Thank you. Thank you for listening to my ranting and raving, my mad and crazed ramblings, and insane ideas. Thank you for listening to me talk incessantly about this book for over a year and yet still responded with excitement. There were times when I wanted to stop, to give up, to put this insane idea away and never touch it again. Thank you for keeping me going.

To my wife Natalie, to my parents, to my sister Autumn, to Ryan, to Brendon, and to many others, I thank you. I also thank you, the reader, for taking the time to read this book. My greatest hope is that this book either gives you something or takes something from you. Only if you walk away from this work unaltered then I have failed.

K. J. Beck
Parts Unknown
March 2021

PARASOMNIA

CHAPTER 1

THE SHRINK

"It happened again."

The words echoed through the silence, bouncing off the cheap carpet and cracked walls before striking the bargain-bin floral paintings that made the place feel more like a hospital than an office. It was a hospital, Leo reminded himself, a single-room hospital shoved in the back of some unassuming office complex.

He sipped his coffee. His breath forcing the steam to bend and curl, forming strange shapes as it dissipated into the stale air. His jeans squeaked against the red leather couch as he shifted his position, crossing one leg over another as he leaned back and closed his eyes. This couch was horrible, uncomfortable for laying or sitting. Shrinks were supposed to have comfortable couches, but this particular shrink must have missed that part of the class. She probably just liked the color. Doctor Ipsom was like that.

"Same time?" Her voice was like steel wool grinding against sand paper. He winced. He would have found a new shrink months ago if his insurance had covered it. Unfortunately, he was stuck with Doctor Ipsom.

He opened his eyes, strands of eyelashes catching and tangling before breaking away. Doctor Marie Ipsom sat near the corner of the room in a hideous mustard armchair that looked even less comfortable than the couch. Her gray hair was pulled back in a too-tight bun. If she pulled it tighter, maybe it would smooth the wrinkles that mottled her otherwise boring and unassuming face. Leo had a hard time imagining her as a younger woman, though the image came to mind of a librarian, shuffling from book to book, terrified of the world. The face remained hers though, long, thin, and wrinkled with age. She was terrible at her job, even as a librarian.

"Yea. 2:30. On the dot." Leo muttered between sips of coffee, his eyes studying the hospital paintings as the doctor scrawled notes in her tiny book. Anything would have been more welcoming than sterile prints of pastel flowers. They clashed with the furniture in the most uncomfortable ways. He took a deep breath. That was just the artist in him, always critiquing color choices, always seeing the discord in inadequate works. God, there were so many bad pieces of art in the world.

"Can you describe to me what happened?" She lifted her eyes from the pages and folded her hands. Dead stare boring into him. The look of a narcissist. Anyone could get a psych degree, and anyone with enough commitment could get a doctorate, though not everyone was cut out for the job. Doctor Ipsom certainly was not, though looking at her you could tell she thought she was the best that ever had or ever would live.

Leo tapped his foot against the carpet, boots beating silently to a rhythm that existed only in his mind. How many times would he repeat the same story to this woman? How could he be clearer than 'it happened again'?

"Well, Doctor. As I've told you numerous times in our many visits, it always starts with that damn ringing."

"The phone?" She interrupted, scrawling more notes in her tiny book.

He sighed and took another sip of coffee, "Yes, a phone. Ringing somewhere in my apartment, plain as day. I can even picture it, build an image in my mind just from the sound. It's an older phone, one of the types that hangs up horizontal, with a rotary dial on the face. One that jacks straight into the wall and doesn't need power. So, I get up, or I think I'm getting up. I never really know, but I always glance at the clock. 2:30. Never a minute earlier, never a minute later. As soon as my feet touch the floor, there's this blinding white light. Hot, like phosphorus behind my eyes. Have you ever heard the color white, doctor?"

She shook her head, eyes studying him even as she jotted more notes into her book, pen scratching like cat claws against the paper.

"It's terribly loud. It's like all the sounds boiled down into one long, miserable symphony of pain. I scream, or try to scream, there's not really sound inside that white... just light. There's a voice. It says something to me. The same thing every night, though I've never been able to make out what it is. It's deep... but... high pitched at the same time. All garbled nonsense, I can't make heads or tails of it. I just know it's not any language I've ever heard. Then the light blinks out, and I wake up. Analog clock by my bed always reads 3:30, and the one on my microwave is always blinking like the power went out. I have to reset the damn thing every morning."

Leo's heart raced. Merely speaking of that nightly experience terrified him. How long had it been since he had slept through the night, or since he had experienced blissful sleep without this same scene playing out?

"And you're certain this phone is not in any adjacent apartments?" Doctor Ipsom asked with complete sincerity.

Leo shook his head, both in response to the question, and in shock at how ignorant this supposed doctor was. How many months had he been seeing her, telling her this same story? How many times would she ask the same questions? She jotted it all down in that damned book of hers, why didn't she refer to her notes? Was she even making notes? He had a half a mind to snatch up that little red book and read it back to her in her own words, but he restrained himself.

"No. I've asked around. No one has a phone like that anymore. The Super said there aren't even copper phone lines in the walls. Said they were ripped out a decade ago when they wired the place with Internet."

She nodded her head. The sound of her pen was the only thing that broke the stale and miserable silence.

"Leo, have you considered the possibility that you might be having seizures?"

He blinked. She had never asked him this before.

"No, well… yea, I guess it's possible. But it doesn't seem very likely. I mean. A seizure at 2:30 every single night that lasts for exactly one hour?"

"Stranger things have happened. Does anyone in your family have a history of epilepsy or brain tumors, perhaps?"

Brain tumors. She dropped the words so matter-of-factly she might as well have been telling him next week's forecast. His heart raced. He tapped his foot even faster.

"Not that I'm aware of. Both sets of grandparents died in their sleep in their 90s, both of my parents are healthy, no issues. Their siblings are healthy too, as far as I'm aware."

The doctor nodded, her bun threatening to bob, but remaining stiff as stone.

"Still, I would like you to get an MRI. You're still taking the medication I prescribed you?" Her tone didn't change, but somehow her voice became more threatening.

No, a librarian was the wrong image, she would fit better as a nun in a Catholic school. He could feel the yard stick striking his hands as she stared him down.

"Yes, every day as prescribed. They're killing my creativity though, doctor. I haven't painted anything in weeks. Clients are getting real heated with me." It was true. Whatever she had prescribed him sapped the life out of him, scrambled his brain up like an omelet.

"They're sugar pills, Leo." Her voice scratched against the inside of his brain. "I wanted to see if this was all in your head."

A small bit of red flared somewhere in the back of his mind. Rage? Anger? No, it was something else. But whatever it was, it was definitely red. He lowered his eyes and took another sip, breathing deep as his foot tap-tapped against the floor. So, the creative block wasn't the medication's fault, it was his own. No, that red wasn't anger. It was fear. Fear that he was slowly losing his mind.

"I see. So, probably more a lack of sleep that's causing issues with my art than anything?" He lifted his eyes without moving his head. The Doctor's face blurred and swirled behind the steam.

"It could be many things, Leo. Right now, the thing to concern yourself with is getting better. Your art will be there. Right now, we need to figure out what is happening at night." She paused, scratching words into her book before flipping it closed and capping the pen. Her frail shoulders fell a bit as she relaxed, inasmuch as someone like her could really relax. The woman was stiffer than a board. He wondered sometimes if she slept standing up, if her muscles were unable to loosen up enough to lie down. The thought of her emerging from a coffin every morning made him smile.

"How is your personal life? Friends, relationships?"

"Normal. Nothing's really changed. A lot of late-night art shows or gallery parties on the weekends. It's all work, really. No relationships to speak of, don't really have the time."

"Any interests or perspectives? Relationships are important to our mental health."

He shook his head and downed the rest of the coffee in a single gulp. "Not since Tori. But we've already talked about that. I'm taking a break from it all for a while, gonna just go solo for a bit. This shit with my sleep is more important than dating right now. I'm barely able to keep my career afloat, much less commit to an adult relationship."

It was true. Since Tori had walked out of his life, he hadn't been very interested in anyone. Sure, there were plenty of gorgeous women around, the art world was full of them. They were like sculptures to him though, perfect, incredible to look at, wonderful to engage with, and then forgot about the moment he turned his back. Tori had been different. He had given her his heart, and she had stomped on it without a second thought. No, that wasn't fair. It was his fault. All of it. He hadn't appreciated her while she was around. He'd let her walk out, watched it happen for almost a year before she finally left, and didn't do a damn thing to stop it.

He glanced down, checking the time on the entirely-too-expensive wrist watch strapped across his wrist. A gift from a banker who had commissioned him for a custom piece. The watch was worth more than the painting, but the man had insisted on giving the gift. Leo couldn't remember the last time he'd taken it off.

"I'm very sorry Doctor Ipsom, I actually must be going. If I don't, then I'll be late. My work is being featured in an exhibition this evening in the National Gallery. They're celebrating local artists. It's a big deal. Biggest deal anyone's made of my work in a while." He smiled, rising to his feet as he fastened the top button of his blazer.

"That is fantastic news Leo." Doctor Ipsom rose from the chair, her mouth curling into what Leo could only guess was her attempt at a smile. "I will see you again next week. Same time. Confirm with Connie on your way out. Please know that I still have to bill you for the full time."

He nodded, he expected nothing less. He pulled open the door revealing an unadorned, sterile waiting room. Tossing the empty Styrofoam cup into a wire waste-basket, he laid his hands on the counter, scanning the piles of billing paperwork strewn across Connie's desk. Her blond ponytail bobbed as she moved papers this way and that, typing figures into her computer.

"Same time next week Mr. Harr?" Her voice was cheerful as she turned and smiled at him. Those eyes. They glimmered like jades. He felt his heart skip a beat. She was the exact opposite of the doctor. All youth, beauty, and energy. He had asked her once if he could paint her, though her reply had been less than desirable.

"I can't fraternize with patients, sir." She had said.

Well. He tried.

"Yes, same time next week Connie, thanks." He managed a smile. The thought of coming back here turned his stomach. He hated this place.

"I have you in the system. And your address has not changed, correct?"

"Nope. Still live in the same place." He nodded his head, his foot tapping once more against the carpet. He paid a fortune for these visits, entirely more than what they were worth. The balance always arrived in a nondescript white envelope. Bad news always seemed to come in plain wrapping.

"Thank you for that information, Mr. Harr. We will send the bill to that address and see you next week." She clicked away on the keyboard, never turning her head.

He drummed his fingers against the counter, tapping his foot in time with his fingers.

"Hey Connie. Offer's still open. I'll find a new doctor if I have to. Your portrait could hang in a museum. No pressure. Just throwing it out there." He smiled, and turned, walking past the row of empty chairs, stepping through the glass doors into the chilly night air. Did he sound like a predator? Maybe he was coming on too strong. He wasn't hitting on her though, he genuinely just wanted to paint her. She had the perfect face for a portrait. How would she know that though? She probably thought he was a creep.

"Stupid," he muttered to himself as he descended the stairs to the sidewalk.

A gust of icy wind tore through the streets, ripping through his blazer. Winter hadn't left yet, and spring didn't seem certain if it was ready to take its place or if it was staying away for a while longer. That was the thing with Washington D.C., you never quite knew what you would get. Ninety degrees in the dead of winter wasn't unheard of, neither were winters that stretched into the end of April. The cold was a nuisance but he didn't look forward to summer, he never did. Clothes sticking to you, the humidity through the roof. Made sense, though. After all, they built the city on top of a swamp.

Leo stepped past a group of tourists, obvious by their wide-eyed expressions as they pointed at every building they passed by, and leaned out into the road to flag down a taxi. How long had it been since he'd taken a taxi instead of a ride-share? His hand slid down, patting his pocket to make sure his phone was still there. There wasn't any time to call one now. He couldn't be late, not tonight. Too much rode on making a good impression. Just one commission was all he needed. Just one and he could finally catch up on his rent. Mr. Russo was getting impatient. The man put up with a lot, but three months behind was bordering on abusive. It wouldn't be long before Leo found himself evicted, out on his ass in the streets with nowhere to go.

A yellow-striped sedan slid up against the curb, *Taxi* painted in large faded letters on the side. Leo pulled open the door and ducked inside.

"National Gallery," he muttered as he slammed the door shut, rubbing his hands against each other for warmth. "There's fifty extra bucks in it for you if you can get me there in seven minutes."

The taxi driver adjusted the rear-view mirror, middle eastern features and blue eyes visibly amused by the request.

"Seven minutes?" He had a faint accent. Was that British? "How about seventy-five dollars and I get you there in five?"

"Done," Leo didn't even hesitate. He glanced down at his watch, delicate gold hands inching towards his demise.

The engine roared, and the wheels screamed, scattering pedestrians like flocks of pigeons. Leo felt the seat swallow him and he smiled. Perhaps today would be his lucky day.

CHAPTER 2

THE EXHIBITION

Leo sipped his drink, some kind of fruity cocktail. Cheap garbage. He couldn't even taste the liquor. Men and women wearing the height of fashion's latest trends milled about him, paying him no mind as he stared at the painting, arms crossed. It reminded him of Escher, except Escher's works had been original. This was a copy of a copy, needlessly complicated, colors clashing in horrific ways. He knew the artist. Her works were always this way. He never understood why people liked them so much.

"It expresses the inner turmoil we all feel. That fear of being lost." She told him; voice trained to sound bored in contrast to her wide-eyed excitement.

"I feel it," he lied before walking her to his own painting. They stopped before it and gazed silently.

Jessie crossed her arms, eyes scanning the work. A nondescript shadow atop a singular rowboat, adrift in a violent, tumultuous ocean. A nearly photo-realistic scene, though each brush stroke had been painstakingly crafted to give an odd surrealist aspect to the painting. It was disconcerting to look at. It sort of swallowed you as you gazed into it.

"Is that me in the boat? Leo, did you put me in one of your paintings?" Jessie smiled.

A middle-aged couple walked by, muttering to each other.

"It's like the artist put me in his painting," the woman said.

"Interesting," the man replied, "I could have sworn I saw my face on that character in that rowboat."

Jessie's smile flipped, thin lips curling into a most unattractive pout. She walked away and Leo smiled. She was a fraud, a hack, like most of the artists present. People who threw paint on a canvas and then made-up stories to define the mess they had made. Jessie was the worst of all though, not a single work of hers was original.

A server glided by, carrying a silver tray of drinks. Leo swapped his empty glass with a full one. He hated these events. Small galleries were fine, they felt friendly. This felt like he was a fish waiting to be devoured by a shark. Everyone was at each others' throats. The artists maneuvering and insulting each other to make themselves look better, dealers sneaking around like snakes trying to get the best deal while ensuring the artists themselves made nothing. It was a shit show. Larger exhibitions always were.

Leo propped himself against a column, eyes glazing over as he stared out into the sea of humanity that moved from one end of the exhibition hall to the other. Here and there he would shake hands with someone who recognized him, but mostly he was a ghost. He preferred it that way. Less pressure.

His eyelids grew heavy as he sipped his drink. Alcohol was not his preferred drug of choice. He usually preferred uppers. Cocaine was the best, though he had chilled out on it recently. He had blamed the night terrors on it and had gone through a hell of a comedown getting off the stuff. How long had it been since he last slept through the night? At least a month. Or was it longer?

Leo rubbed his eyes with his free hand, pressing his fingers into the sockets until the fuzzy white lights behind his eyes morphed into blotches of green and yellow. He smiled, thinking about the bottle of sugar pills in his jacket pocket. Doctor Ipsom thought she was clever, but he had a suspicion early on those pills weren't doing anything, and had supplemented them with even more caffeine. It would be a short time now before he crashed and crashed hard. Perhaps when it finally happened, when his body couldn't take it anymore, when it gave up and turned off, perhaps then he could sleep through the night again. All he really wanted was some cocaine.

"Mr. Harr!" A male voice with an accent somewhere between British and pretentious asshole rang out from behind him. He knew exactly who it belonged to.

"Ah, Mr. Alpert, how good it is to see you." Leo lied, smiling as he turned towards the fat man, leaning in as they exchanged kisses on the cheek.

He hated this pleasantry, especially with men like Alpert. The man smelled like a whorehouse, from the cheap perfume to the sin and despair. Round face slick with sweat, he wore a silk suit more expensive than anything Leo could ever hope to own. The few hairs remaining on his head were slicked back with what appeared to be Vaseline, though Leo knew better. Jordan Alpert would have paid a small fortune to ensure his balding head looked precisely how he meant it to. That's how the man worked, spending fortunes on everything and noticing none of the money flying out the window. He was an art collector, one of the wealthiest and most affluent in the city. Some said he had high political ties, though Leo wondered if it had more to do with his talent for procuring illegal goods for politicians rather than his latest opinions on foreign policy.

"Your piece is absolutely stunning. What gave you such inspiration?" Alpert's voice rang out through the hall like a discordant gong, at odds with any harmony and lacking musicality.

"I guess you could say I was in a dark place. That person on the boat, that's me, you, anyone really. Aren't we all just lost in a raging sea?" Leo took a quick sip from his drink to hide his frown. He hated this man, more than any other collector he had ever dealt with.

"Right you are, right you are. Leo, I'll cut to the chase. I want to commission a work from you. Something different from your normal pieces. I'll pay you handsomely."

"You'll pay upfront?" Leo's eyes never left Alpert's. He had heard this song and dance the last time he did a painting for Jordan Alpert. It had allegedly been for a client of his, though the client never paid, and Alpert claimed it wasn't his responsibility to cover the costs. Leo never got the painting back. Thankfully, he had half-assed the work. Only a few nights lost.

"I regret that our last dealing was less than satisfactory to all parties." Alpert smiled wide, his yellowed teeth reminding Leo of some predatory animal.

"What ever happened to that painting?" Leo glanced around the room as he sipped his drink, searching for any way out of the conversation. He would rather be destitute than rely on Alpert's money.

"I ended up finding a buyer, eventually. They were extremely excited to acquire the piece. They commended you on your incredible work."

Leo turned back towards Alpert, looking the man up and down expectantly.

"So, where's my cut?"

Alpert smiled wide, "Well you see Leo, our agreement was all tied to the original buyer. If you read your contract in full, you would see that I owe you nothing regarding any other sales of the work."

A flash of red erupted somewhere deep in Leo's mind. A glow that swallowed up the other colors, humming with a subsonic bass that shook his core.

"You mean, I don't get a dime for my work?" Leo felt his hands shaking. The red pulsed and quivered, the bass rose and fell.

"I'm sorry Leo, but that's business. Now enough about that, I want to discuss this new piece I would like to commission from you. You see, I imagine a…"

The voice faded; the red had swallowed up almost everything; the bass threatened to drown out the sounds of the gallery.

"Alpert, you can take your offer and shove it far, far up your ass." Leo turned in time to see another waiter coming by with drinks. He swapped his empty glass with a flourish.

"Leo, now don't be like that." Leo could hear Alpert's smile.

The red was everything. The bass shook the very floor beneath his feet. Leo turned, and leaned in, his nose inches from Alpert's fat face. From here he could smell the sweat and the grease. It was nauseating.

"Alpert. I said fuck off."

Without waiting for a reply, he stormed off toward anywhere else. He didn't trust himself not to knock the piece of shit square in the teeth. Alpert deserved it. Hell, Alpert probably deserved a lot more than that.

Leo wandered the exhibition, gliding past fellow artists, collectors, museum curators, greeting them all in the most professional manor he could muster. Thankfully, Leo Harr wasn't exactly known for his tact or professionalism. People didn't look down upon him, but they knew what they were getting when they saw Leo. Art was the only important thing. The pleasantries just got in the way. Some people appreciated that though, and he had heard more than a handful of whispers behind his back about him being a genuine artist. Unfortunately, it didn't put food on his plate or pay his rent. He still needed to sell his works.

The crowds dwindled, and his vision grew increasingly fuzzy. How many drinks had he had at this point? How much time had even passed? He looked down at his watch, but couldn't make heads or tails of it. *Shit*, he thought, *I'm drunk*.

"Leo." a musical voice, like a harp crossed with a flute drifted through the air and settled into his ears. His heart raced as he turned towards the most beautiful woman he had ever met. Lucille Barett, an artist herself, but also a collector. She came from money. Her father ran one of the most affluent auction houses in the country, and she herself managed a small gallery here in the city.

He smiled, struggling to remember words as she glided towards him. Black cocktail dress accentuating every curve. She was the perfect silhouette of femininity. Curly brown hair fell below her waist, bobbing with every step of her bright red stilettos. Deep hazel eyes peered out from her heart-shaped face, piercing his soul and threatening to bring him to his knees. Bright red lips curled in the faintest smile. She knew what she was about. She knew how she looked.

"Lucille!" He exclaimed, leaning in, both exchanging kisses on the cheek. He didn't much mind this pleasantry with her. His mind wandered to far-off places, places filled with lusts and violent passions.

"Your works continue to impress me Leo." She accentuated every word perfectly; her voice was pure professionalism. He felt out of his element for more than one reason. Her looks alone were enough to make him feel inadequate, but the way she carried herself merely enhanced that insecurity.

"You have no idea how much that means to me." He wasn't lying. From her, any compliment meant the world.

"I would like to purchase your work. The one you're displaying here tonight."

Leo stuttered, uncertain what to ask for the painting. He had a number in his head, but suddenly it didn't quite feel right. Her eyes begged him to lower it, her voice cooed at him to give it away for a kiss. He took a deep breath, and then the alcohol took over.

"You can have it," the words fell from his lips before he could retake control of himself. "Hey, could I take you out for dinner one of these nights?"

Reality crashed down upon him. Words he wished he could retract were now forever out of reach. He had drunk too much. This was why he didn't like booze. It made you say stupid shit. He hoped he wasn't slurring his words; he hoped she hadn't noticed that he was drunk.

Lucille smiled and crossed her arms, resting her chin in her hand as she gazed into his eyes.

"Oh Leo, how long have we been doing this?" She sounded flirtatious. Was she toying with him?

"Pardon?" He swallowed hard, pushing down the regret as far as he could.

"We dance around what we both know is there. Professionalism and work trapping us in this waltz that keeps us out of arms reach." She leaned in and pressed her finger against his lips. "I can't tell you how long I've waited for you to ask me out." She bit her lip and winked. "Let's skip dinner. My place. Tonight. I'll meet you out front in an hour."

With that, she turned and walked off. Her heels clicking against the stone floor. Leo realized he was shaking. He could hear the blood pumping in his ears. Had that worked? Had that really worked? He blinked and glanced around the room. No one seemed to have noticed. The entire thing felt like it had lasted an eternity, but it had probably only been a second or two.

A server walked by and Leo grabbed a fresh glass, downing it in a single gulp before placing it back on the tray. The waiter frowned at him, but Leo only smiled. He wanted to yell out; he wanted to whoop and holler down the halls. The sleeplessness and exhaustion had disappeared, and for the first time in a long time he felt like a million dollars.

CHAPTER 3

THE CALL

The taxi bounced down the street, stopping and starting abruptly at each red light. Leo felt his stomach churning, both from the vehicle's terrible lurching, and from nervousness. He had drunk entirely too much and now he regretted it horribly. He glanced over at Lucille; her face illuminated by the glow of her cell phone as her thumbs tapped away message after message. For her, work never stopped. Leo admired that about her. If she wasn't creating art, she was selling it, and if she wasn't doing either of those, then she was sleeping. Art was her life; it was her everything.

Leo swallowed hard as the cab slammed a pothole, bouncing him out of his seat as he nearly struck his head against the roof. Lucille chuckled and clicked her phone screen to black.

"Oh Leo," she cooed, turning towards him as she leaned her back against the door. She slid her feet out of her heels and ran them up his calf. He hadn't felt a woman's touch since Tori walked out on him. He hadn't realized how much he'd missed it.

"You've really been waiting for me to ask you out?" He smiled, playing it as cool as he could manage. Inside, he felt like a hurricane was raging. Emotions and hormones flowing through him like some kind of horrible drug cocktail.

Lucille laughed. "Leo, don't play dumb. There's always been chemistry between us. Unfortunately, you and I have always been… otherwise occupied, so to speak."

He nodded, an image of Tori's smiling face flashing across his vision. Even months later, it still felt like he was cheating on her.

"Yea, Tori and I had been together for a while." He hoped his voice didn't sound as sad as those words made him feel.

"And I was building my business, working my way to the top." She made the final 'p' pop like a balloon. Her lips curled into a sly grin at the insinuation they both knew was there.

Lucille wasn't easy, but she knew how to use what she had to get what she wanted. She hadn't built her career strictly on her artistic and business talents, but she wasn't shy about that fact, and Leo appreciated that. To her, her body was just another asset. He couldn't blame her. If he had curves like her, he would use them for the same reasons.

"I do hope you understand that our little… adventure this evening has nothing to do with business. In fact, I refuse to accept the painting for less than market value." And just like that, she was all business again. The sexually playful banter replaced with serious professionalism.

"Lucille, really–" Leo started, but she leaned across the cab and placed her finger on his lips. Her eyes were brown crystals, infinite pools of eternity that swallowed his words and threatened to devour him.

"Leo dear. Enough about business." With that she grabbed his lower lip between her teeth, and everything was overwhelmed by a violent shade of blue.

He knew the driver was watching; he caught the man's glances in the rear-view, but he didn't care. Let the man watch, hell, let him film it if he wanted to. Leo Harr was on top of the world, and he didn't give a damn who knew about it. Time was an irrelevant construct, drifting between shades of blue and violet as their bodies and mouths intertwined. He could see down upon himself, watching from above as the taxicab streaked through the city, leaving a red trail of taillight in its wake.

An instant and an eternity later the taxi stopped, and Lucille detached herself from him, snatching her stilettos from the floor of the cab and winking his direction. Leo could think of nothing else but her. If the world ended in that very moment, he wasn't certain he would have noticed. He reached into his pocket and pulled out a bill. Grant's face stared back at him and screamed that it was entirely too much money, but Leo paid it no mind and handed the driver the fifty.

"Keep the change, man," Leo chuckled as he slapped the driver on the shoulder.

In one swift motion he swung open the door and leapt from the car, jumping up onto the sidewalk as he snatched Lucille by the waist and pulled her in for another kiss. She laughed, throwing her head back as she placed a finger on his lips and *tsk'd* at him.

"Inside."

Everything was blue, his blood, his vision, his heartbeat. It coated the world in a thick shimmering shade of sticky tar. He noticed the front of her home, an actual home and not an apartment. The thing must have been worth over a million, but he didn't care. The stone front, the marble stairs, the statues at the entrance, he paid attention to none of it. Another time it would have overwhelmed him, but not now, not with the blue coursing through his veins.

Passing through two massive doors, they entered a gaping hall with double spiraling staircases rising from a mirror-polished marble floor that wrapped up and around to the second story. It reminded him of something out of the Great Gatsby. Leo wasn't unfamiliar with the trappings of the exceedingly wealthy, but he had never expected Lucille to live in a home such as this.

"Wait for me, I'm going to slip into something…
more comfortable." She licked her lips and glided up the
stairs, casting glances behind her shoulder that held more
meaning than words ever could have.

It was all cliché, the entire situation, but he didn't
care. It was silly for her to change when he was just going
to strip her naked as fast as possible, but it was part of the
game, and for her he would play any game she wanted.
Taking a deep breath and cracking his neck, Leo turned towards one of the hall's adjacent rooms, pushing open a
large white door as his feet fell upon crimson carpet.

Paintings hung across the walls, paintings of all
styles and colors. He recognized most of them as Lucille's
work, though there were others scattered among the col-
lection. He smiled as his eyes fell upon one of his paintings, one of his first. A field of red roses against a violent
stormy sky. It fit entirely too well in this room. Had she
chosen the carpet because of this painting?

Leo chuckled to himself as he noticed the red
couch. Not like the one Doctor Ipsom had in her office.
No, this one was different, this one was stunning. It was the
color of fresh blood, dark and tantalizing. It didn't clash
with the carpet, and its curves were a perfect analogue for
Lucille herself. Leo unbuttoned his blazer and fell into the
couch. It was comfortable. Too comfortable. If he stayed
there too long, he might fall asleep. He could feel his mind
swirling from the alcohol. If he could only get a few minutes of sleep. No, the blue was still with him, he would be
fine as long as he had the blue.

Somewhere in the house, from another room, a clock ticked the seconds away. The ticking echoed through the home, each second tearing through the silence. The blue threatened to flee as anxiety crept in upon him. He hated the silence, but he hated the clock more. That perpetual reminder of his own mortality. Leo shook his head. No, not the time for that now, not the time. He closed his eyes and tried to picture Lucille naked. He only got as far as removing her black cocktail dress before a phone rang.

He knew that ring.

His eyes snapped open, and he jumped to his feet. The blue fled, dissipating like smoke as first a flash of red, followed by the darkest blackness crept into his mind. Time slowed to a crawl.

Ring, ring.

He could picture the phone. Rotary dial with a receiver rested horizontally upon its top. It wasn't necessary to check the time; he knew it was 2:30.

Ring, ring.

Creeping across the crimson carpet, he slid towards another door. The brass knob felt like ice against his clammy skin. For a moment he thought he could see his breath.

Ring, ring.

Leo pushed the door open. It felt like someone had punched him in the gut. He couldn't breathe, he couldn't do anything. He was petrified, paralyzed as his eyes fell upon a rotary phone, yellowed from age, resting atop an oak end table.

Ring, ring.

He moved towards it. No flash of light had crippled him or thrown him to his knees in blinding pain. There was no voice calling to him from the recesses of his own mind. But something was there, something that pressed down on him, an external force compelling him to pick up the receiver.

Ring, ring.

As he stared at it, eyes wide and heart racing, he realized there was no light in this room and yet he could see. The phone itself emanated some kind of glow. It wasn't white, but it wasn't the normal yellow of a halogen bulb. He couldn't describe it, but he could see it, feel it. It was more of a knowing than an understanding, more of an idea of light than the actuality of it. There was no phone line plugged into the phone. Nothing connected it to the wall.

Ring, ring.

Leo reached a shaking hand towards the receiver. The blackness in his mind swallowed up all other emotions. He had never felt so afraid. His fingers wrapped around the plastic, and in one swift motion, he pulled the receiver to his ear.

The surrounding light blinked out. There was nothing but the phone hovering in the darkness, floating in the nothingness. Static crackled in his ear, static and a voice. He recognized that voice. All bass and all treble at once, an impossible sound that vibrated through his core. He felt the words in his chest.

"Leo Harr," the voice said his name like a question. This was the first time he had understood it.

"Yes," he confirmed. He was no longer shaking. In fact, he was no longer doing anything. His body was somewhere else. Here he was an idea of himself, a separate entity yet wholly himself at the same time. This place, this black place devoid of anything save that yellowed plastic phone, was everything and nothing.

"We have been trying to–" Static burst forth, followed by a faint ethereal chorus of words that weren't words. "You have been resisting us."

Leo didn't reply. He didn't know what to say.

"You... the perpendicular... complex array... danger... beware the red door... await further instruction..."

Static roared through the receiver, deafening him though he dared not put it down.

"Danger? What are you talking about?"

"Contact will be made... silver horse... white cube... black sphere... silver horse... white cube... black sphere... silver horse... white cube... black sphere..."

The voice repeated those words over and over. Leo screamed into the receiver, but his voice was silence in an eternal echo.

"Silver horse... white cube... black sphere..."

The voice echoed on and on. Static screamed at him. The ethereal chorus chanted in the background.

"Silver horse... white cube... black sphere..."

A pinprick of light grew in the blackness. Whiter than white itself. Leo yelled with all he had. He tried to throw down the receiver; he tried to run as the white light swallowed the darkness. The pain, he knew that pain. Not again. The sounds faded into the white. The white consumed everything. Phosphorus behind his eyes. The sound of white burrowed into his brain, tearing his humanity from his soul as it scoured him with its perfect brightness.

Leo was no longer Leo. He was an animal. A primal instinct. The pain was everything, the sound of white burned with the icy cold of death itself. He couldn't hold on much longer. The white threatened to consume him, shredding him into infinite pieces as it scattered his mind across an eternal universe of nothingness.

He snapped up, gasping for air. Everything was black. There was no sound save for a faint ringing in his ear. He was panting. Sweat soaked through his shirt and the sheets. The smell of piss was heavy in the air. He glanced around, uncertain of where he was. This place was familiar. Too familiar. Where had he been when it all began? Lifting his hand to his forehead, he wiped the sweat away. He couldn't remember anything.

Leo reached over and clicked his phone on, the screen blinding him as his eyes adjusted in the darkness, illuminating an analog clock whose face seemed to have shattered. There was glass everywhere.

3:30 mocked him from his phone screen.

He sighed and collapsed back into his bed. His bed. Yes. He was home. He had pissed himself though, he would need to do laundry in the morning. There was a feeling, a faint half-memory that he should be somewhere else, but it was just out of reach. His muscles ached. Everything was exhaustion. His eyes fell closed, and the ringing in his ears subsided as he drifted off to sleep.

"Silver horse… white cube… black sphere…" The words echoed on and on and on…

CHAPTER 4

THE CHECK

How long had it been since he'd drank that much? Leo shook his head as he took another long sip from the now-warm energy drink. He had stripped the bed bare, the sheets and his clothes from the previous night had been soaked in piss. Leo sighed, taking another long drink from the crinkled aluminum can. His head throbbed like someone was beating it with a hammer.

Before him lay a stack of mail, but he paid it no mind as he rolled his head back into the couch. Something bounced around inside of his head, some faint half-memory. He had been at the exhibition, and then what? He couldn't remember anything. There had been faint red lipstick marks on his face when he awoke, and he vaguely remembered a woman's voice, but he couldn't place any of it.

The sunlight pouring in from the windows seared the inside of his eyes, making him feel like a stranger in this world. The last time he'd blacked out had been in college, and that was off straight liquor. Unless someone had drugged him, there was no way he had blacked out from drinking watered down mixed drinks at an art exhibition. Leo rubbed his temples, straining for a memory, reaching out for some faint recollection that could help him understand what had happened.

All he remembered was hearing the phone ring. Had he picked it up this time? Grinding his teeth in frustration, he clenched his fist around the can. The sound of crumpling metal echoed through the apartment. Drops of caffeine-laden sugar-water fell from newly torn holes, dripping all over the couch. He didn't care. He hated that couch.

Leo rose and tossed the can into the garbage, then retrieved a wet sponge from the sink. Cursing under his breath, he scrubbed the drink out of the couch's fabric. He would have left it there if his apartment hadn't been notorious for ants.

It was a small place, a studio apartment with no dividers to break the bedroom space from the kitchen from the living room. Leo liked it that way, though. Every space was for everything. A perfect living arrangement. There was no difference if he painted in the kitchen or the living room. It didn't matter if he slept on the couch or the bed. It was all the same room.

Dozens of paintings, in various stages of completion, were scattered about the place, some resting on counters or tables, others on easels with dried and crusty pallets laying nearby. Some even still had wet paint on them. Each of those paintings represented a month's rent he would never see. No one would buy these, these were too different, too strange. He never planned on showing them to anyone. It was more of a personal project, an artist's journey, than anything else.

A beep startled Leo, and he jumped to his feet. For a moment he wobbled, his head spinning as his brain struggled to deal with the unfamiliar sensation of being upright. Another beep echoed from the screen pad at his door. Someone was trying to get in from outside.

Rubbing his eyes, he moved towards the door, tossing the sponge into the sink as he passed. The screen showed a camera view of the main entrance. This system was a way for tenants to know who they were letting in without simply trusting a voice. It had, at one time, been an audio only feed, until a rash of break-ins forced the Super to upgrade the security system.

Lucille stood perfectly in frame, her eyes flickering between the camera and the door. His breath caught in his throat. Even in this grainy camera feed, she was gorgeous. Another buzz jolted him back to reality. Without a thought, Leo hit the button to unlock the front door. He watched her turn towards the camera and wave, winking before disappearing from view.

In a flurry of frantic energy, Leo grabbed clean clothes and changed as fast as he could, cleaning up trash and loose items while he hopped into his jeans. The sheets were in the wash, so he didn't need to worry about that. He just hoped the entire place didn't stink.

Just as he was about to grab a can of air freshener, a rap at the door stopped him in his tracks. He glanced about the room, running his fingers through his hair before unlatching and opening the door.

Lucille stood before him, a picture of perfection, tight jeans hugging her legs, accentuating her curves like ocean waves. She stood there, brown hair falling free around her shoulders, with a hint of mischief on her face. Leo always thought her facial expressions were somewhere between inappropriately sexual and indescribably taunting.

"Hey," Leo's eyebrows wrinkled in a confusion that matched his tone, "I didn't expect to see you here. Ignore the mess, I was just cleaning up."

She chuckled as he motioned for her to enter. She glided past him like a queen surveying her realm, black heels clicking against the hardwood floor.

"You left this behind last night." A smirk crawled across her face.

She tossed his wallet onto the counter, then continued towards the nearest unfinished painting.

Leo shut the door softly behind him as he stared at the black leather wallet. It was his, but why did she have it?

"Last night was interesting," Lucille chuckled as she crossed her arms and stared down the painting as if going to war with it. Leo had never gotten used to the way she analyzed artwork. It was aggressive and sometimes downright hostile.

"Yea, hey, I'm really sorry if I did, or said anything. I think I blacked out last night." Leo scratched his head as he moved up next to her, his eyes falling on the unfinished work. It was an embarrassment to have her see these.

"Oh sweetie. I'm glad it happened the way it did. We both had a bit more to drink than we should have. When I came downstairs and saw you asleep on the couch, I was actually kind of relieved. There's always another time," she winked at him, "but last night would have ruined it."

His mind swirled. Had he and Lucille almost... no, certainly not. Sure, he had been enamored with her for years, ever since he had moved to D.C. but who wouldn't be?

"Speaking of, I owe you for that painting." She turned and faced him, hazel eyes drowning him in hormones and emotion. He was putty in her hands every time she looked at him, though she had never taken advantage of it. Strange, that he had seen her use her gift on many a man, but she had never tried it with him. He had always thought of her as a close friend, even though the tension between them was incredible. He could have lived his entire life never getting closer to her than he had, but it seemed as if he had done something, and perhaps now they were drawing closer than either had expected.

"Painting? Which one?" His eyes darted towards the half-finished piece before them.

"Oh Leo," her voice was mocking but also heavy with genuine concern, "you really did have too much to drink last night. The one from the exhibition. I offered to buy it from you, and since you never came back to collect it, I've... well... I've already taken it home." She laughed, her voice a musical song.

"Wait," he put his hands up and shook his head, "how did I get home last night?"

She *tsk'd* him then moved towards the couch and sat down, crossing one leg over another as her eyes scanned the host of unfinished works before her.

"I came downstairs, and you were fast asleep. I couldn't wake you, and trust me, I tried." She winked again. What on earth did that mean? "I called a ride for you, took you back here, used your keys to get us in, tucked you in and kissed your forehead and went home myself. It was only after I awoke this morning that I noticed you had left your wallet. It must have slid out of your pocked while you slept."

Leo shook his head. "Why don't I remember any of this? I know I couldn't have drunk that much, not at some art exhibition at a damned museum."

The playful facade fell away and Lucille's concern grew. It was as if the angel had fallen to earth and become human. Expressions, tones of voice, and movements that she had practiced to the point of perfection slid away, leaving bare the woman beneath. He wanted to smile. This was the Lucille he truly loved.

"Do you think someone drugged you?"

Leo shrugged. "Perhaps, but I don't know why."

A smile crept back across her face. "I could think of a few reasons."

There it was again, that hint that something had happened. Why had he been at her house, anyway?

"It's probably just me. I get nervous and, well, you know, I drink more than I should at those things."

"It was more fun when we used to do lines in the bathroom together. You become kind of a downer when you drink." She was serious, and he knew she was right. He and alcohol did not get along very well.

"I had to stop; I wasn't sleeping at night." He still wasn't sleeping at night.

"Wouldn't have anything to do with this would it?" She motioned to the paintings surrounding them. "How many times can you paint a telephone?"

Leo's eyes moved from one painting to another. Each a different representation of what he thought the phone from his nightmares might look like. Red, black, blue, some had rotary dials, others had buttons, some hung up horizontally on top of the base, others looked like phones from the 90s, their ear pieces sliding into the base itself. None of them had been correct though, that's why none of them had been finished. He always got to a point and then stopped when he realized it just wasn't right.

"Yea, actually it does," he muttered under his breath. There was a sudden feeling that if he tried to paint the phone at that very moment, he could finally do it.

"Don't get me wrong, they're beautiful, but I'm not certain that anyone is in the market for retro telephone portraits these days." Lucille chuckled and rose from the couch.

"You never know. Heiresses are always getting portraits done of their damn dogs, maybe one really loved her phone." Leo faked a smile, though he was certain Lucille could see right through it.

"Well, I like them, but I like your other works better. Can I keep this one?" She nodded towards a painting that felt as close as he had ever managed to the real thing. Everything about the painting had felt right except the color. He knew for certain now that it wasn't baby blue.

"Sure," he replied with a shrug. He was just going to throw them out, anyway.

She smiled as she snatched it from the easel and glided by him, rubbing her hand against his cheek as she moved towards the counter. "Speaking of which, here is the check for that painting. I'm going to leave it right here. Don't call me later and tell me it's too much, this is what I'm paying and I won't take it back." She slid a check from her pocket and folded it in half so he couldn't see the amount. "As for last night. Everything I said was true. The alcohol just helped me say it." Again, the facade fell away. Her eyes betrayed a vulnerability he had never seen in her before. Leo didn't understand what she was referring to, but he felt as if he didn't need to know. Her eyes said everything.

"Same here." He swallowed hard, hoping that he hadn't said anything stupid.

She smiled, a genuine smile, before the mask fell back into place. "Good, then I expect you to take me on some proper dates. You know, there's that place that everyone talks about. The one with the candles, I can never remember the name. Friday?" She asked it like a question, though he knew it wasn't.

"Friday," he replied, his lips curling into a smile as the hormones flooded his system.

Her heels clicked against the wood floor as she moved towards him. She threw her free arm around his neck and kissed him deep. Just as he was falling into it, she pulled away, winking and biting her lip as she glided towards the exit.

"Friday it is," She said, pulling the door open and disappearing into the hall without another word.

He stared after her as her footsteps faded, trying to understand what had just happened. The woman was an anomaly. She was like a ghost, floating away before betraying too much of herself. She had always been that way, but today he had seen more of her true self than ever before. He shook his head. Was he in a relationship with Lucille Barett? How on earth had he managed that? Maybe he needed to drink more often.

Shaking the thoughts from his head, he moved towards the counter and grabbed the folded check. As he unfolded it, his heart stopped. Written in black ink, in the flowing script that was uniquely Lucille's, was the exact amount left on his lease. He clenched his jaw as his emotions swung between excited, grateful, and furious. It was too much money, especially from the woman he was now apparently romantically involved with. No, he wouldn't be taking handouts. He would not be another one of her toys whom she paid to keep around. Then again, it was kind of nice to know he didn't have to worry about being evicted anymore.

Clutching the check in his hand, he fell onto the couch. Whatever he had done at the exhibition had made his life exceedingly more complicated than it had been. He shook his head. What else did he expect from getting mixed up with Lucille Barett?

CHAPTER 5

THE CONVENIENCE STORE

Leo walked the empty sidewalks, head down, jacket pulled tight against the blistering winds that buffeted him. He cursed under his breath each time the cold bit through his clothes, latching its icy teeth into his skin and causing him to shudder involuntarily. It was supposed to be early spring, but winter would just not go away. Someone had tried to explain D.C.'s weather patterns to him, but Leo simply replied with, "So, what you're saying is, it's all bullshit?" That had put an end to any further discussion.

There was a spring in his step, a jolly gait that made his high spirits visible even at a distance. He hadn't felt this good in months, maybe even years. It had been three days since Lucille had visited him at his apartment, and three nights of solid sleep. He hadn't heard that cursed color white in three wonderful days.

The only problem was that itching in the back of his head telling him there was something important he needed to remember. No matter. He pushed it aside with ease. Anything was better than living in that horrible sleep-deprived haze. He had started painting again, really painting. He felt like this might be a renaissance for his work, and now that his rent was covered, maybe he could start putting money in the bank.

Leo lifted his hands to his face and warmed his palms with his breath, rubbing them together to force away the cold. Just a few more blocks and he would be warm again, at least for a bit. He cursed himself under his breath for even coming out into the cold to start with. An urge he had been fighting against for weeks finally won out. He had decided that, for the first time in years, he would buy a pack of cigarettes.

"Stupid" he muttered under his breath.

It was a reward in a sense, a reward for finally sleeping, a reward for painting again, a reward for being happy. Yes, that's what it was, and he deserved it.

He rubbed the roof of his mouth with his tongue. He could already taste and smell the smoke. He hated that smell and he hated the taste even more. That had been part of the reason he had quit. The other had been the breathing. What use was it to be fit, healthy, and young if you couldn't run a block without coughing up black tar?

He rounded the corner, still arguing with himself, still trying to talk himself out of it. The convenience store stood before him. 'Joe's Deli' the sign read, glowing in neon red that flickered as if the lights would burn out at any moment. A cherry red Mustang sat out front, parked illegally against the sidewalk, its windows tinted so black they were nearly opaque. It was still running but he couldn't tell if anyone was inside. Leo stared at it as he stepped into the store. He had always wanted one of those. The owner had taken incredible care of it too. The thing was so clean you could eat off it.

The bell dinged as he stepped through the door, and his skin tingled from the sudden warmth. It wasn't exactly hot, but it was warmer than outside and free from the wind, and that made it warm enough.

Leo walked straight to the counter. Not another soul wandered the store, a strange thing for a Friday, but Leo paid it no mind. People did what they did, and it was no business of his. He realized he didn't even know what time it was. Perhaps the people who worked regular jobs weren't even awake yet. For him, time was all the same. Night, day, noon, evening, it meant nothing save for the amount of artificial light he had to pump into his apartment. He wondered for a moment what it would be like to work a normal job, to have a schedule, deadlines, people that needed you to be places at certain times. Maybe that's what hell was like, someone else owning all your time.

"Hey Leo, how ya been?" The fat, balding man behind the counter had a voice that sounded as if he was perpetually fighting a cold. Leo imagined that even after a shower and wearing fresh clothes the man would still be covered in a sheen of sweat. No matter the weather, Joe was always sweating profusely.

"Hey Joe. Pack of Camels, and… yea a lighter too."

Joe raised an eyebrow as he retrieved the items and slid them across the counter. "You smokin' again? Business that bad?"

Leo snickered, retrieving a crumpled-up bill from his wallet. "Business has never been better. Just sold a piece, paid for the rest of my lease and then some. How are things here?"

Joe grunted as he took the bill and popped open the register. "You can see it for yourself. Everyone's all about natural and healthy shit now. They don't buy smokes, they buy those electronic things instead. They don't want my sandwiches because I use mayo and shit on it, they want all that vegan crap."

He dropped the change into Leo's hand and slammed the register shut, a physical period at the end of his sentence.

"I have a theory, Leo. One day we're gonna find out that this vegan shit is worse for you than the real thing. Everyone wants to eat low fat, but they're eatin' a shit ton of sugar instead. They tell their kids not to eat a damn lollipop 'cause it might give 'em ADHD while they bury their faces in single packs of yogurt that's got more sugar in it than a quart of ice cream. You got people out there sayin' cigarettes are bad while every day they're blowin' through a carton of 'em in the form of some rechargeable pen lookin' thing.

"Here's what I think. I think those little pens they're smokin' are all gonna blow here one day, just explode in their faces while they're usin' 'em. I think these vegan burgers everyone's about, it's gonna come out they've been using meat the entire damn time. That or everyone's colons are gonna burn away from the inside out from all the chemicals. I think everyone's gonna lose their shit here real soon."

Leo slipped the unopened pack and the lighter into his jacket pocket and leaned against the counter. He liked Joe. He rarely agreed with Joe, but the world needed people like Joe. They were a sanity check on the rest of society.

"Why don't you just start making healthier sandwiches and selling vape pens?"

"Eh, I got a big order coming in, gonna re-brand the hell out of this place. But it's the principle of the thing, Leo. Someone asked you to paint some dumb shit but offered you a bucket of cash to do it, I bet you would, but would you be happy?"

"No." He had done that before, and he certainly hadn't been.

"Exactly. Here's the thing, man. Everyone's driving around in electric cars, eatin' veggie burgers and usin' vape pens to save the environment, every single one of them thinks they're a fuckin' Captain Planet or some shit. But you ever ask yourself, what happens to all that battery acid when the batteries burn out, or the plastic when the vape pens stop workin'? I mean, it's gotta go somewhere? They don't ship it to space, they bury it somewhere far away and pretend it isn't gonna be a problem in a few years.

"That's someone else's planet, you see. It isn't their problem because they don't have to look at it anymore. Doesn't matter if it leaks into the water, it isn't their water, that's someone else's water. All this save the world garbage, it's feel-good self-righteous bullshit.

"Those fake meat factories are pumpin' out shit like you wouldn't believe. The chemicals they gotta use in the food, you end up shittin' it out, it goes back into the water. Fuck man, you're drinking more birth control and hormone supplements in your water than you'd even like to believe. Now you got dirty water and the fish are all fucked up, but no one seems to care about that. Then what happens when we got too many damn cows running around that no one's eatin'? We gonna just kill em off and not eat em?

"I'm sure the PETA folks are gonna love that. They wanna save the animals, so they put em back where they came from and instead of savin' anything, now they're just killing each other like they always have been while a family of poor folk are starvin' to death because they can't afford the cost of the veggie burgers. I don't know Leo; it's all kind of a shit show you know?"

"Eh I wouldn't worry too much about it, Joe. In a few years we're all going to be living on Mars, anyway," Leo chuckled.

"Oh, don't get me started on that shit." Joe's voice reached a new pitch that threatened to rattle the stock off the shelves. His eyes settled on Leo's face, narrowing as they caught the sarcasm. "I see what you're doin' you bastard. You always get me riled up. I love ya, but damn if you aren't gonna give me an aneurysm one of these days."

Leo laughed and slapped his hand down on the counter.

"Always a pleasure Joe, take care of yourself. Have fun with the veggie burgers!"

"Oh, fuck off," Joe laughed in reply.

The bell dinged and Leo stepped back out onto the sidewalk with a smile on his face. The icy air bit into his skin, but he didn't feel it as badly as before. Joe was a good person, rough around the edges and full of bad takes, but the world needed more Joes, and Leo was happy he knew one.

He passed by the red Mustang, engine still purring as it sat in the same illegal parking spot as before. For a moment Leo thought about letting the owner know before the cops came around and hit them with a ticket, but he thought better of it and crossed the street. He couldn't be certain what kind of person was behind those tinted windows, and he didn't have the energy to deal with it.

It was part of Leo's way of looking at the world. Not everyone was a Joe, some people were Jims, and Jims were the opposite of Joes. You call a Jim out on something, do something nice like let them know their car might get towed or let them know they're illegally parked, and a Jim would be liable to start a scene.

Jims are wound too tight. People always think it's the Joes who are wound too tight, with their loud voices, their overuse of profanity, and their general angst and distrust of the world, but it's the Jims who are really wound too tight. A Joe might get loud and yell about electric cars and veggie burgers, but that's just how he expresses himself. A Jim on the other hand, a Jim would key your diesel truck because they believed you were killing the planet, or protest a beef company out of business because they thought they were doing some good while hundreds of people lost their jobs as a result. Jims were the real pain in the ass.

The problem is that sometimes Joes look like Jims and Jims look like Joes. You never quite know who is who until you cross some invisible line. A Joe might beat your ass, then offer you a smoke and a beer, whereas a Jim might say nothing, and then the next thing you know your boss is calling you into his office and firing you because an anonymous source sent them some Tweets you posted when you were thirteen and, poof, career gone.

Leo reached his hand into his jacket pocket and grabbed the pack of cigarettes. Hesitating, he put them back and instead began blowing heat into his hands. That pack of cigarettes caused him fear, an inordinate amount of it.

He had quit smoking years ago, but that craving had crept up on him in this bitter cold. There was just something about smoking a cigarette with an icy wind biting at your face. Winters were always the hardest for him, even now, even years later. The sole purpose of his journey had been to pick up this pack of cigarettes to "just have it around. In case." That was his reasoning, that was how he justified it to himself.

It was a humorous situation. If someone had offered him a bump, he wouldn't have thought twice, but he had been back and forth on this pack of cigarettes for weeks. It was the principle of the thing. He had conquered this vice, and he would not allow it to take him back. Except that in a way it already had. He could feel it pulling him down like a sack of bricks, the nearly weightless pack of cigarettes that rested so perfectly in his jacket pocket.

Leo rounded the corner and pulled out his keys. He would be happy to be back inside, warm and painting. He craved it.

His keys rattled as he alighted the steps to the apartment entrance. A sound caught his attention, a low rumbling, like thunder, but more abstract. He turned his head to see the cherry red Mustang parked about a hundred feet from the apartment entrance, illegally blocking a fire hydrant.

He wrinkled his forehead and blinked a few times. The silver horse emblem caught his attention for some reason, itching the back of his head as if it held some sort of importance. He shook the thought away, but instantly another thought took its place. Was he being followed? Adrenaline shot through his veins as he unlocked the door with shaking hands and slid inside. He slammed the door behind him and made certain it was locked.

Why would someone be following him? He relaxed and chuckled to himself, turning towards the row of mailboxes and checking his for mail. Empty. No one had any reason to follow him. It was just him being paranoid.

Still nervous, but in better spirits, he began his trek upstairs towards his apartment. He realized he had been clutching the pack of cigarettes in his hand the entire time. No, no need yet. Perhaps he was still not caught up on sleep. Yes, that was it. That had to be it.

CHAPTER 6

THE VISIT

Leo entered his apartment and slammed the door shut behind him. Placing his keys, wallet, and newly purchased cigarettes down upon the counter next to Lucille's still un-cashed check, he let out a lengthy sigh of relief.

There were days when the idea of interacting with the outside world was unbearable, where the mere thought of social contact pressed down upon him like a vice. He had ideas, pictures, images, scenes, concepts, dreams that he needed to tear from his mind and cast upon the canvas before they ate his brain from the inside out. These things were like parasites, slowly gnawing away at his sanity unless he extracted them and cast them into the world proper.

He removed his coat and tossed it upon the bed. No sooner had the jacket struck the mattress did a beep scream from the security pad. He sighed once more, his eyes darting between the screen and his half-finished work. Perhaps it was Lucille. The very idea set his blood aflame with a flood of endorphins and hormones. Almost overeager, he rushed towards the screen, heart pounding with excitement.

It was not Lucille. Instead, a strange-looking man in an all-black suit wearing a large-brimmed, and rather out of place, brown cowboy hat stood before the entrance like a statue. In his right hand he held a cubic white bowling bag. An image flashed in the recesses of Leo's mind. An image of this man sitting inside that red Mustang. But no, that image was merely conjecture. The windows had been tinted far too dark for Leo to see who drove that machine.

As Leo stared at the screen, the man reached up and pressed the ringer once more. Another beep tore through the silence of the apartment. Leo lifted his finger to the pad and engaged the microphone.

"Who is it?" He asked, his voice a blend of curiosity and annoyance.

The stranger turned his head towards the camera and smiled. The man was entirely too plain. No features upon his face would burn into Leo's mind, no matter how he stared at the man. Were this stranger to turn and walk away now, Leo would have no way to describe him to anyone who might ask. Against this plainness the cowboy hat now seemed grotesque.

"A friend," the man replied. The smell of ozone filled Leo's nostrils. It smelled like the start of an electrical fire.

"I don't recognize you, and I don't want what you're selling." This man's features were disconcerting, but Leo couldn't take his eyes away. The plainness was almost inhuman.

The stranger merely smiled and bent down, placing the bowling bag upon the ground. With one fluid motion he unzipped the bag and retrieved a perfectly black bowling ball, which he lifted towards the camera.

A flash of memory exploded inside Leo's mind. The image of the silver emblem upon the red Mustang, a horse rearing on its hind legs. The cubic white bowling bag, the black bowling ball. Words formed, words he felt he had heard before but could not place their origin.

Silver Horse... White Cube... Black Sphere...

Without thinking, Leo slammed his hand against the screen and buzzed the man in. What was going on? He felt dizzy and disoriented. It was as if the world itself was folding inside out and he was in the center. Like the light was bending in a massive kaleidoscope and he was flipping around like the beads and the confetti; his image distorting and stretching upon the mirror walls of his own mind.

He sat down upon the bed, the smell of ozone still heavy in his nostrils, and placed his head in his hands. He tried to remember; he felt like he had to remember, but there was nothing to grab hold of. Everything was a fragment of a fragment. The image of a telephone hung suspended in his imagination, a yellowed plastic thing that taunted him.

A soft knock at the door startled him, and he snapped back into reality with a jolt. Leo moved towards the door, his hands shaking as he grasped the knob and pulled it open. That strange man stood before him, taller than he had seemed on the screen, taller than any man Leo had ever met. He stood nearly seven feet tall. Without waiting for a greeting, the man slid inside, somehow pushing past Leo without touching him, though there didn't seem to be enough room to do so.

The stranger examined the room, muttering to himself as his eyes noted every detail. He dropped the white bag at the foot of the bed and then removed his cowboy hat, placing it upon the counter. The man was entirely bald, though he appeared too young for such a thing to happen naturally. Leo blinked; in fact he couldn't tell how old the man was. Nothing about him stood out in any way. The plainness was the only thing he would remember about this fellow, and that plainness was so perfect that he could distinguish nothing about the man's identity.

"Who are you?" Leo's voice was nearly a whisper as he struggled against the increasingly powerful stench of ozone that wafted through the air.

The stranger lifted a hand to stop Leo and continued searching the room with his eyes. "Has anyone given you anything recently? Anything to hold on to, to care for?" The man's voice was also plain, but there was an authority in it that demanded Leo's obedience.

"No," Leo replied, "nobody's asked me to hold on to anything. What is this about?"

The stranger visibly relaxed and his mouth curled into a slight smile as he moved towards one of Leo's half-finished paintings.

"We will never get used to your geometry," he muttered as his eyes flickered from the painting to the couch to the corner of the room where the ceiling and two walls joined.

Leo stepped forward, his eyes never leaving the stranger. There was no feeling of danger from this man. He did not worry about being attacked, or that this was some lunatic he had let into his house. The voice was familiar, too familiar in a way. He knew he had heard it before, but he could not place where.

"Do I know you?" Leo's eyes narrowed as he struggled to remember.

The stranger smiled. "No, you do not. But we know you. Well, in the sense than any can know any other. We have no name, but you may call us 'They'. It is the only conceptually viable reference which may on one hand explain our state of being and on the other hand express relation to your own."

Leo took a deep breath and sat down on the edge of the couch. His trepidation was now replaced with curiosity.

"Okay They, I am Leo Harr. You say you know me already. What brings you into my home?"

They peered into Leo's eyes as if he was looking for something. His eyes slid up and down Leo's face as one would study a sculpture or an interesting artifact of a past civilization. After several silent moments, They shook his head and smiled.

"This is to be expected. You remembered the access code else you would not have admitted us into your home, yet it seems you remember nothing else. Unfortunate, yet insignificant. Have you been having any experiences that may be identified as bright, loud, and uncomfortable?"

Leo nodded his head slowly, "Yes, every night at 2:30 a phone would ring, but there was no phone. I would get up to answer it and a white blinding sound and light would burn the back of my eyes until it faded at 3:30. Hasn't happened for a few days now though."

They nodded. "Would you say it stopped when you answered the phone?"

"Answered the phone?"

"Yes, after our conversation, once we made contact with you. Would you say it stopped after that?"

Leo shook his head, his eyes widening as he shrugged in confusion, "I don't know what you're talking about."

They nodded and retrieved a pill bottle from the inside of his suit jacket.

"It's called the Afterbleed, a condition of fractured time. Think of it like radio interference. It is difficult to send signals across the Break, and unfortunately even more difficult for those of the Double Helix to receive them without some sort of extreme discomfort. These will help with the Afterbleed, though. Take one of these every day and you will no longer experience such discomfort. It will cleanse the signals."

They tossed the pill bottle to Leo, who snatched it from the air and turned it over in his fingers as he examined the strange oblong shapes inside.

"Look man, I don't know you and you're in my house giving me strange drugs. I want to know what this is all about." Leo set his jaw and locked his eyes upon the stranger. Something knotted in his chest.

They nodded and lifted his wrist, his eyes falling upon a plain silver watch face set into a black band. "Yes, of course. We only have a short amount of time. Coming to you in this form is difficult, these Reality Boxes are quite fragile and degrade at a rapid pace." The stranger moved towards Leo and sat on the far side of the couch, his eyes studying the walls and the corners of the room. "What is the name your kind use for the strange geometry here?"

"Euclidean." Leo blurted out without a thought.

"So very strange." They muttered under his breath. "Leo do you recall this?" With that, the man retrieved several photographs and laid them on the couch cushions between them.

Leo nearly gasped. Each picture was of him, some taken from outside and some taken from inside a home. He remembered that night well. It was the night after Tori left and there had been a massive party at his friend Lon's home. He looked through the photos, reliving the night as it devolved into a drug-filled stupor. It started with cocaine, then went to mushrooms and ecstasy and LSD, and whatever happened after that he couldn't remember. He always associated that night with the color red.

"Have you been spying on me?" Rage coursed through his veins, a rage that threatened to erupt upon this stranger in a flurry of blows.

"Not in the way you think. We took these photos before we came here. Retrocausal-Photoimagery. No one was outside the window nor inside this home when that night occurred, though we pulled these images from that night as if they had been. It is more than we can explain in our first meeting, we are afraid."

For some reason the anger subsided, and Leo felt a calm wash over him. It made sense, but he wasn't certain why. In reality, none of this made sense, it was all madness. This mentally ill stranger, who called himself 'They' and spoke of himself in the plural, had been stalking him and was now in his home. No, that wasn't what it was at all. It was something more, though he could not understand why or how he knew it.

"We are short on time so let us explain it the best we can. On this night you crossed the Break into the Underlower, a place beyond the Lower, a place that has been sealed away. In this place are housed those who unraveled their Others, those who seek to unravel all the Others. Somehow, and we do not understand how, you punched a hole in this door. We fear that some of those in

the Underlower are now able to cross the Break. We fear
they can now move into this plane. If they can access the
Transit, then nothing stops them from moving beyond,
into the Lower, or the Upper, or even the Neverafter. We
cannot see into the Underlower, and so we cannot see what
it was you did to break that hole in their door. Only you can
undo what you have done, and we fear there is little time."

Leo wanted to laugh out loud. The man sounded
insane. Lower, Underlower, Neverafter. It sounded like the
mad words of a Disney film writer. "Look man, I think you
need to leave, I have no idea what you're talking about, but
you don't seem to be doing well… mentally."

"Your world, your here, now, then, will be, it is the
Transit, the place beyond the Break. The corridor of travel
between the Others. The Others do not touch each other,
yet each Other touches the Transit beyond the Break. This
has been and will always be the lane to navigate between
the Others, or what you would call dimensions. You have
become a Perpendicular, like ourselves, or like the telephone. You are now something that intersects between the
Transit and the Others in a more active way than those of
the Double Helix generally do.

"Whatever you did, breaking this hole into the
Underlower, it threatens the Others as well as the Transit.
If they break through that hole, if they can move along the
Transit into the Others, they can unravel them one by one
until there is nothing left, just as they unraveled their own
before. We, and those from the Others, sealed away these
Unraveled else they would have destroyed it all. No one

blames you for what you did, as no one understands how you became Perpendicular to start. We simply need your help to fix what you have broken. Will you help us, Leo?"

Leo's smile faded as he gazed into the eyes of this strange man. He could see it now in the plainness of his features. This was no man at all. This was someone's idea of all men, a picture of every man combined into a portrait so plain that it would be recognizable to all as human. In this portrait he saw the truth in this stranger's words. It sounded like nonsense, but the memories of the recurring nightmare and the impossible photographs that lay before him told him it was something else.

"What do I have to do?" Leo asked, as he lowered his head and studied one of the pictures. Taken from inside the home itself, it showed him with a rolled dollar bill stuffed up his nostril as he inhaled an incredible amount of cocaine off an oak table. He would have remembered if anyone had taken this one. This was how the night had started. He had still been sober when it happened.

"We don't know," They rose and checked his watch again. "We are working on that now. The important thing is that you are open to helping us, that is a start. We will contact you again, though we cannot say what form that contact will take. Take one of those pills every day so you can receive the call. The Afterbleed can be a terrible thing for those made of the Double Helix. It will destroy you over time, and we cannot allow that to happen.

"You may keep these photographs, we only brought them along to prove to you that we are who we say we are."

They retrieved his cowboy hat and bowling case as he moved towards the door. He turned back, his eyes piercing into Leo's soul.

"Beware the red door. Be on your guard and be careful. The Unraveled could be anywhere. We do not know how many have crossed the Break. If we could locate you, then we have no doubt that they know who you are as well." With that, the stranger pulled open the door and disappeared into the hall.

Leo let the photograph slip from his fingers as he rose to his feet. Without thinking, he moved towards the counter and wrapped his fingers around the pack of cigarettes. Tearing the cellophane from the container, he slid open the box and pulled a single white and brown cylinder from the package. With one hand he placed the cigarette in his mouth and with another he grabbed a lighter. The sound of the lighter igniting rang through the silent apartment, and Leo took a long deep breath of smoke as he closed his eyes and contemplated his sanity.

CHAPTER 7

THE PILL

Leo stared down at the translucent bottle of pills before him, his eyes studying the orange-tinted oblong tablets as he buttoned his shirt. He had stared at this bottle throughout the day, studying it in the haze of cigarette smoke as he ran through the strange meeting in his mind. There were but two possibilities: either he was going insane and that man, this bottle, and that meeting were merely side effects of a creeping psychosis, or the strange man was telling the truth.

It was hard for him to accept the idea that he was psychotic, even though the recurring nightmares and general paranoia seemed to prove the fact. Doctor Ipsom believed it was a tumor. It would explain most of what he had been experiencing. Even still, he couldn't accept it. There was something too 'real' about it all.

He found it equally difficult to accept that he had been visited by a being from another reality, that he had somehow broken a hole in a door to some evil parallel dimension, and that he, Leo Harr, was to be the savior of them all. It sounded like something out of a kid's book, or a dreadful story.

Leo shook his head and snatched up the unmarked bottle of pills. Taking one of those pills could go a long way towards proving which of the two possibilities were true. If it helped the headaches and blinding light, then the man was telling the truth. If it poisoned him or sent him into a drug-induced coma… well, then he might end up dead and none of it would matter anyway.

Shaking the bottle, he popped the safety cap. He reached two fingers inside and plucked a single oblong shape from the pile before replacing the cap and laying it back upon the counter. Turning the pill over and over in his fingers, he looked for the identification imprint. There was none. This pill was entirely unmarked. It could be anything from Ecstasy to Anthrax. He wouldn't know which until he tried it.

Lifting the pill to his lips, he hesitated. In mere moments a car would arrive, and inside of that car would sit Lucille Barett. Tonight was an important night for them. Tonight was to be their first official date. What if this pill sent him into a spiral? He shook his head and tossed it into his mouth, swallowing it down with a gulp of saliva. It was too late now. Lucille was important, but knowing whether or not he was losing his mind was more so.

A steady buzzing erupted from his coat pocket, vibrating against his skin as it rippled over and over in a rhythmic pattern. He fumbled for a moment before his hands clasped the phone. Lucille's name stared at him in large sans-serif font. He answered.

"Hey," he surprised himself with how confident he sounded. In reality, he was all nerves and anxiety.

"I'm out front," her voice sang through the speaker, tickling the inside of his ear.

"Be right down." He hung up. He hated phone conversations. Thankfully, Lucille did too.

Leo snatched his keys and wallet from the counter and exited his apartment, only stopping long enough to lock the door behind him before continuing down the stairs to the entrance. His breathing marked out seconds and his feet clicked in the space between them. The smell of time was in the air, a smell that marked the infinity between one moment and the next, a smell that wafted in from outside the minute and second hands and permeated the voids between, filling them with possibility.

His fingers tingled as he reached towards the car door. For a moment, a tension gripped his heart. Fear that the pill he had ingested was some kind of poison or psychoactive substance washed over him. What if he died in her arms? What if she watched his mind eaten from the inside out by some hyper-concentrated form of LSD? The fear abated as he pulled open the door and the smiling face of Lucille greeted him, her head resting against the window of the black sedan, her hands folded beneath her chin. He smiled at her and her smile grew larger in response.

Time was electric in the air, as if some great storm was ready to descend upon the town. He felt like he was made of electricity, like he could ride those winds of time that whipped through the street, etching faces into brick and pocking holes in steel as they moved without care or purpose. In one breath he felt as if he saw the city as it had been, and in another he felt as if he saw it as it would be. He felt alive.

Leo swung open the door and jumped into the backseat, joining Lucille who immediately called directions out to the driver. The car sped off, pulling Leo into the leather. He smiled. He could feel the correlation between speed and time as if it were one. Breathing deeply, he inhaled that sweet time smell, the smell of forever and now, the smell of always and never. It had a strange resemblance to upholstery cleaner.

"Never thought we would actually end up doing this," Lucille laughed, her eyes twinkling at him as she scooted closer and placed her head upon his shoulder.

"Me neither," Leo replied, leaning his head against hers and closing his eyes. She smelled like flowers.

The car jerked as the driver swerved to avoid a cyclist tossing Leo and Lucille to different sides of the vehicle.

"Share the road, you damned idiot!" The driver yelled, his gruff voice booming through the calm like thunder.

The picturesque scene flipped on its head. The wonderful smell of possibility became the existential dread of mortality. The clocks that had moments before represented eternity, now chipped away at his remaining moments on earth, slowly counting down until one day he would be nothing but dust. Leo swallowed hard. This was not a psychoactive trip. He had done enough drugs to be certain of that. These were his own chemicals, produced by his own body. Hormones had crafted that euphoria of possibility, just as they now produced this terror of mortality. He ground his teeth and clenched his fists. He could feel the speeding vehicle tearing through the streets, he could see the angels of death keeping pace with the car as they waited for the driver to make some fatal mistake.

"Leo, are you alright?" Lucille's eyes were wide, she had been studying him.

He nodded, his neck stiff, his muscles tight. Was he losing his mind? Was he truly psychotic and only just now realizing it? Was any of this real at all?

"I'm okay. Just tired. I haven't been sleeping well." He managed a crooked half-smile, but it did little to lessen the concern on her face.

"Leo, what's going on? You've seemed stressed lately." Gone was the sexuality, gone was the flirtatiousness. In that moment, they were merely two humans doing their best to get by.

"It's nothing. Let's just enjoy tonight. I've been looking forward to it." The smile was genuine this time, and after a moment of concerned investigative stares, Lucille smiled back and placed her head back upon his shoulder.

"I've been waiting for this for so long," she whispered. Her voice held no sexual promise, just a bare desire to be loved. In that moment Leo felt sorry for her in a way he never thought he would. Here was a woman whose perfection even the gods themselves would worship, and all she wanted was love. Genuine love. Not one night's love, not love with caveats. Just love. He ran his fingers across her palm and closed his eyes. It was all he wanted too.

In the blink of an eye, they were sitting across from each other in the restaurant, their faces illuminated by candlelight as a pianist played softly in the corner. The curves and perfection of Lucille's face were the only thing that Leo saw as he stared into her hazel eyes. She blushed and looked away; he smiled but kept looking. Did he love this woman? It was too early to say for certain, but the hormones coursing through his veins screamed at him to take her to bed. He wanted nothing more.

"How's work been?" Leo asked between bites of salmon. The food here wasn't the best, even though it was the most expensive place in town. Food wasn't the reason you came here though, it was the atmosphere, the experience.

"Oh Leo, let's not talk about work." Lucille rolled her eyes and gave him a look of severe disappointment.

"Okay, okay, sorry," he lifted his palms in surrender, "What do you want out of life?"

She stopped mid-bite and merely stared at him. The question had caught her off guard. Good.

"Let's talk about work," she smiled, then proceeded to explain how well the business was doing. She had purchased and sold a significant number of works, and business was going better than ever. Leo let the words fall over him, though he paid little attention to the details. He just enjoyed hearing her voice.

"And what about you? You say you aren't sleeping. I come by and you have dozens of telephone portraits painted around your apartment. You're on edge lately and don't think I haven't noticed. What's going on with you?"

This time it was Leo's turn to pause. He should have known better than to play games with someone like Lucille. She always won, that was just the rule.

He breathed deeply, then realized he had been tapping his foot against the leg of the chair. Forcing himself to stop, he smiled, placing his utensils down and folding his hands across his lap.

"It's only fair you should know," he began, his voice lacking any of the confidence he had feigned moments before. "Every night I've been having the same dream. Well, most nights. 2:30 I wake up to a phone ringing somewhere in my apartment, but there's no phone, none anywhere in the building. I get out of bed and this blinding light, this painful, blinding light burns and burns. Suddenly it's gone and I look over and its 3:30. I visit a shrink by the way, don't know if I've ever told you that."

He paused.

Lucille merely chuckled. "We're artists sweetie, we all see shrinks."

"Right," he continued, "well, she wants me to get a brain scan. She thinks I might have a tumor or something. The dreams went away for a bit, something happened, I can't remember what, but they stopped. Then earlier today this... strange guy shows up at my door." He stopped and swallowed hard. Should he continue? The story until now was fairly bland and could be attributed to stress or even withdraw. Lucille knew about his love of narcotics, and she had her own dalliances with them herself. Bringing up this stranger, that was another level of insanity. What would she say? Would she call the police and have them haul him away somewhere? No, Lucille wouldn't do that. He had to trust someone, and if there was anyone he knew he could trust it was Lucille. "So, he came around, seemed to know a lot about these dreams I'm having. But what he said was insane. Look, please don't judge me for what I'm going to say, okay? If I'm crazy, just tell me. Please?"

Lucille placed her utensils down and stared deep into his eyes. "I promise." Her words were soft, but he knew they were true.

Leo took another deep cleansing breath before he continued. "He said a bunch of stuff about other worlds, like other dimensions or something. He used weird words for them though like Others, and he called our world the

Transit. You remember that party at Lon's house? After Tori and I split?"

Lucille nodded and smiled, "You got seven different kinds of fucked up that night."

"Yea, well he said I broke something. Apparently, I let in something or broke a door to another dimension or something, I don't even understand what he was saying. He said I need to fix it, but didn't tell me how. He had pictures of me Lucille, pictures from that night, pictures inside and outside the house. I don't know how he got them. Some of those moments I remembered clearly and the angle of the pictures were just... wrong. Like I would have known if someone had taken them, they were taken from inside the room. He gave me these strange pills. Said they would help with the headaches and the blinding light. Something about clearing the signals. Lucille, I know how this sounds, but I've been holding on to this, and I don't know who else to tell. It's crazy, right?"

She replied with silence as she studied him, her eyes staring deeply into his. He felt each drop of sweat emerging from his pores. His foot was tapping again, he didn't even bother stopping it this time.

"Did you take the pills?" Something in her tone of voice caught him off guard. It was not accusatory, it was not judgmental, she was simply curious. Did she believe his story? There was no way she could think he was not insane.

"Yea, I took one before I left to come here." He looked around the room nervously. The candle felt like a spotlight bearing down upon his face. He felt like he was in an interrogation room and the walls were closing in around him. All that existed was Lucille's face, flickering in the candlelight, and the piano music, that haunting piano music, echoing through the nether like a pipe organ singing a dirge.

"And how do you feel?"

The simplicity of the question snapped him back into reality. The piano was no longer haunting but beautiful, the waiters and waitresses moved around in the lanes between tables, the soft conversations of lovers and business associates tickled against his ears.

"I feel fine." He snatched up his fork and tore a sizable chunk out of the salmon.

"I mean, there's a lot of crazy people around. Maybe he was just homeless." She shrugged and continued eating, her stern expression replaced by a soft and welcoming smile.

He stared at her in response. How would he respond if the tables were turned? Would he really say anything? Would he really comment about someone's mental state when they were seeing a professional already? Maybe she thought he had a brain tumor. Maybe she thought he was a junkie. Would he have been so calm after hearing someone he cared about speak such insane words?

"Leo," her voice was stern again, though her smile was more than sexual, "Leo dear, everything is alright. Don't let a stranger ruin our evening. You aren't crazy, you just need a good night's sleep."

Anxiety was building inside of him, and he could not understand why. He was losing his mind. That was the only explanation for any of this. Here he was, on a date with Aphrodite herself, and he was more concerned about some balding, plain-faced nut-job than anything else. Leo nodded his head and smiled, doing the best he could to appear calm and collected. Beneath the table, his foot *tap-tapped* against the floor.

CHAPTER 8

THE TRIANGLE

Waves of color crashed upon the inside of his eyelids, forming shapes that were instantly forgotten as he sailed along the glassy black waters of the void. Silence mingled with the sound of every memory. He felt like he could reach out and take any piece of his life and relive it, but he had no desire to, not tonight.

His arms paddled along in that tiny rowboat, yet those arms were not his own. The tempest that raged around him did not so much as rock his tiny craft. He was immune to the violence. The silent storm did not care about him, and so he did not care about that silent storm.

Leo looked back and saw a lighthouse, its torch flickering in the night, illuminating the waters, warning of rocks to those who would travel in such weather. He smiled as the lighthouse faded and all was darkness once more. Someone had sent him a text or tried to call. The lighthouse itself wasn't real, not any more than anything else here was, but he knew enough to understand that the light might have been. This place pulled from the real world in strange ways, ways it had taken him decades to understand.

He had a sense that he might be sleeping; somewhere in his mind he knew that he was. Time flowed backwards, then rapidly forward; the storm subsided before returning with a vengeance. He was in the space between awake and asleep, a place he was all too familiar with. Tonight, this place had taken on the form of that painting, the one he had sold to Lucille. Her body appeared over the water, a glowing perfect Christ with arms outstretched. Paddling along undisturbed, he dared not reach for her. Something like that might suck him back into a dream, and he was comfortable where he was.

He had once tried explaining to a friend about this state of half-sleep where he could hear the ticking of the clock, understand what was happening around him, and yet compose exceptionally vivid dreams from thin air. That friend had looked at him like he was insane. Apparently not everyone understood this place. No matter. This was his place, and his alone. He could transform it to whatever he desired, move mountains, dry entire oceans, tear the heavens asunder. Everything, all power that ever was or could be, was his.

The paddle struck the black water, gliding through it with ease. He focused on that sound, that perfect, wonderful sound. Every droplet a musical note that together created the most perfect orchestra ever assembled. Leo sighed and looked towards the sky. The black ocean greeted him; it was above him, as it was below him. The sight should have caused him concern, yet he merely smiled. All was as it should be.

Thunder boomed in the distance, rippling the waters and rocking the boat back and forth. Leo grabbed the edges of the tiny vessel and turned to face the sound. Again, the thunder roared, closer now. Waves crashed against him, lapping into the boat and soaking his clothes with frigid water. His heart raced. Something was wrong. He imagined a calm sea again; he imagined the unspoiled void of glassy black water, but nothing changed. Again, the thunder rolled, and this time he watched a massive wave creeping towards him. It would capsize his vessel. It would pull him under. He held his breath and closed his eyes.

Leo shot straight up in bed, gasping for air. Somewhere in the apartment a phone rang. Taking a deep breath, he turned towards the nightstand and picked up his phone. *2:30* stared back at him. So, he was back to this again it seemed.

His eyes darted towards the counter. He couldn't see the pill bottle, but he knew it was there. He had been doing just as the stranger asked. One of those pills a day for almost a week. They were supposed to make the pain go away; they were supposed to take away that horrible screaming white.

The phone rang again; it was somewhere near the couch. He clutched the sheets in a white-knuckled grip as he prepared himself for the searing pain and blinding light. It would be best to just get it over with. Best to just put his feet on the ground and let it wash over him as it burned him from the inside. It wouldn't be any better if he waited. Best to just rip off the bandage and let it happen.

In one swift motion he swung himself out of bed, his bare feet striking the cold, wood floor. He winced in anticipation of a blinding light that never came.

The phone rang once more. So, the stranger had been right. The pills worked. Footsteps echoing softly in the apartment's silence, Leo made his way towards the sound. He could picture it, just like he could picture the images in his half-asleep dream. It wasn't a tangible thing, but it was real enough to him. For a moment he wondered if he was still dreaming.

"Shit!" He cried out as his toe struck the edge of the couch. The popping joint shouted out in time with the phone's ringer. Pain tore through his foot and up his leg. He knew he had broken his toe, but he dared not stop to check. Instead, he limped forward towards the sound, cursing under his breath.

The phone appeared before him out of thin air. It was as if someone had pulled it from his mind and placed it there as some tangible representation of his own perception of reality. The yellowed plastic device hovered in the air at eye level, glowing from inside of itself with a light that was not a light, suspended by nothing. It broke the very laws of physics, but something about it seemed right. Suddenly the very idea of that phone sitting upon a table or a desk seemed maddening and incongruous.

The phone rang again, and Leo snatched up the receiver and placed it to his ear. Something boomed beneath his feet, a sound that lived in the inaudible frequencies below bass and underneath reality itself. Everything about him blinked and in the fraction of an instant he found himself somewhere else. Receiver still to his ear, he looked around.

He stood in a hallway flooded with a strange purple and black light. Everything was reflective, too reflective. It was a hall of mirrors, yet the reflections did not reflect things that were or even could be. The reflections were merely part of the construction, braces that held the structure together, strands worked into the fabric. He looked down; he had no reflection, and neither did the phone that hung before him, suspended impossibly in the air.

The hallway was one long triangle, pulled out and stretched as if it had gone through an extruder. It rotated as it pulled away until the top was the bottom and the bottom the top, creating a perfect void of black in the shape of an inverted triangle. It was so close he felt like he could reach out and touch it, yet he knew if he started towards it, he would never reach it. Something about the angles was upsetting. There was no way that he should see that black void so clearly, not the way the shape itself rotated around on its way towards the terminus. Edges should have been obscured, points lopped off, angles obfuscated, but they were not, and for some reason he could not fully grasp, it all made perfect sense.

Purple light pulsed and static rang through the receiver, chirping along in some incomprehensible rhythm. A voice broke through the static, a voice he recognized as not a voice at all. It was a feeling, a vibration, a color. An orange gradient that faded into neon pink. It spoke in hexagons and tesseracts, and he understood every word.

Not a hole... the door is open... cracked...

Goosebumps rippled across his skin. The voice sounded panicked, terrified. That orange and pink gradient pulsed in time with the surrounding purple. Darkness rippled around the edges like tangible smoke. He understood it. The great darkness of fear.

Must be shut... not sealed... the red door... beware... red door... beware...

Leo's hand was shaking. This fear was not his own, but the fear of a universe, the fear of a collective more powerful than he could imagine. What could strike such fear into something like this?

The void triangle before him began to rotate, though it never moved at all.

Await further instruction...

The triangle unfurled like a flower in bloom. The perfect black of its petals opening wide to reveal an even deeper blackness within. Was this the source of the voice? Was this non-shape, this un-color alive?

Continue dose...

Never had he seen a darkness like this. Was this the void of hell that preachers warned of? Except he felt no fear as he stared through non-Euclidean space into its gaping maw. This blackness was a color, a color he could not comprehend because he had never seen it. His mind shattered as if some kind of reducing valve had broken and the entirety of understanding was now available to him. The colors in the room did not physically change, the cones and rods in his eyes would not allow it. Yet in his mind he could understand. Everywhere there had been black was now alive with color beyond his wildest imagining. The void before him now rippled with a vibrant beauty that threatened to send him to his knees weeping. He could never explain it, no one would ever understand, but it didn't matter. He understood it, now, in this non-place that existed outside of whatever he understood as time. He understood it and he saw it, and that was enough.

C Major... Elm... Turquoise Shell...

A tear rolled down his cheek. This was not for him; this was never meant for him. This place, this existence, this was not meant for him to understand. Yet he did. Every sunset he had ever seen, every clear starry night, everything of earthly beauty faded to ash and drifted away. Color would never be color again, beauty would never exist, not for him, not anymore.

The triangle furled in on itself as the hallway collapsed. He felt the sensation of incredible speed as it rushed towards him and pulled him away at the same time.

He screamed out, begging to stay, begging for them not to take that beauty away from him. His voice was nothing, he was nothing, even that place was nothing. The walls rushed in and there was the sound of static. The smell of ozone filled his nostrils.

In less than an instant, in an impossible span of time shorter than the blink of an eye, he was back in his apartment. His hand was still up by his ear, but it held nothing. Darkness surrounded him, but it was meaningless now. Black, white, red, green, blue, they were nothing, just pale imitations of another world that existed somewhere else, somewhere beyond an invisible wall. The stranger had called it the Break. Suddenly Leo understood exactly what that was. Suddenly he understood all of it.

Leo sighed and walked back towards his bed. His toe throbbed, it definitely felt broken, but he didn't pay it any attention. Instead, he laid back down and stared at the ceiling. A hole existed where his soul had been, a gaping hole that he knew he could never fill. Everything had been stripped from him in that place, everything that had made him human was gone. What was he now that he had seen what he had seen? Still human, nothing could change that. Though now that he understood what that truly meant—now that he understood how small and insignificant he was—how could he continue?

He closed his eyes and tried to picture a placid ocean of black glass, but all he could see was the impossible shapes and colors seared into his mind. Even now they seemed to fade, the memory of them, the comprehension slowly transforming them into shades of oranges, pinks and blues. He rolled over and stared towards his unfinished art piece hiding somewhere in the dark. Color, his colors, the colors he could see and understand were merely representations of true color. He understood that now.

Somewhere in his apartment a clock ticked the seconds away. Each second counting down towards the moment he would eventually expire. Never before had he understood so perfectly the concept of eternity, and in his understanding he suddenly felt so very, very small.

CHAPTER 9

THE SPIRAL

Paint chips flaked from his fingers. Splatter from a half-finished painting he had covered over with coat after coat of pure white. It wasn't right, not anymore. There was something else he had to paint now, something more important.

The smell of yellow filled his nostrils. He knew that smell all too well. The smell that indicated his current position atop a razor's edge as he traversed the minefield of self-destruction. On either side of him cooed the siren song of a psychological spiral, pulling him towards the void below. A beautiful pastel yellow. A warm and welcoming color like the holy fire that struck down Michelangelo's Paul on the road to Damascus. "Pick up your cross and come follow me," it beckoned to him. Empty words, though so tantalizing and difficult to resist. What if this time they were true? What if this time they saved him? He licked the inside of his teeth. He could almost taste that holy kerosene of the cocaine washing him of his sins.

"Leo?" Doctor Ipsom asked, her voice even more grating than before.

He scraped another fleck of white paint from between his fingertips and watched it fall to the floor. It disappeared into the carpet in an almost taunting metaphor; a reminder of the parts of himself that had been left behind in this very room. Maybe he could find his sanity in that cheap brown carpet. Maybe if he sifted through all the dust trapped in those synthetic fibers, he could pick up the pieces and make everything right again.

"Leo? What's wrong?"

He didn't want to look up; he didn't want to reply. Instead, he scraped off another fleck of white and watched it dance as it moved on the air currents, falling like the first autumn leaf. A gorgeous symbol of impending death.

"Leo?" Her voice was louder now, sterner.

He nearly smiled.

"Yes, doctor?" Flakes of white flew from his fingertips like sparks.

"Why wouldn't you answer me, Leo?" She was audibly frustrated. Not an excellent thing for a psychologist to let on to her patient. This woman was truly the worst.

"Nothing personal." He scraped the last piece of paint from his palm and leaned back. That terrible red couch swallowed his body, threatening to hold him there until the sun went supernova or the universe went cold. "The colors in this room are so abrasive. You have horrible taste. Have you ever thought of getting a designer in here? It's no wonder all your patients are insane."

"I beg your pardon?" She was not nearly as offended as she let on. Something in the tone of her voice sounded almost amused. Even the idea of her laugh made Leo grind his teeth. It was a thing he hoped never to hear.

"I'm just saying. The colors are not very relaxing. I feel like, as a shrink, you should have a space that relaxes your clients. This place has always done the opposite. I'm always on edge when I'm here." He looked back down at his hands. For a moment he could almost see the strands of DNA that made up his existence. He blinked and stifled a yawn.

"Have you still not been sleeping well?"

"I haven't been sleeping at all as a matter of fact." He lifted his head and met her gaze. What would she do if she had seen what he had? The image of her eyes melting from her skull flashed before him. Someone like her couldn't have handled gazing into the vastness of eternity.

"Have you still been having that dream?" The scratching of her pen against paper reminded Leo of a hissing snake.

"Not a dream." He looked back down towards his foot. Inside of his shoe was a swollen black and blue toe. Not a dream at all.

"And why do you think that, Leo?" He could tell from her tone that she thought she was making headway. What a fool.

He leaned back in the couch, eyes staring through her with such intensity that she stopped writing and shifted in her chair.

"Let me ask you a question instead doctor. Why are you so certain that it is a dream?"

"Well," she began, flipping through her pages, "I quote, 'No one has a phone like that anymore. The Super said there aren't even copper phone lines in the walls. Said they were ripped out a decade ago when they wired the place with Internet.'" She paused, waiting for some reaction. "You said that in our last visit Leo. So, if there is no phone, then it must be an auditory hallucination or a dream."

Leo licked the inside of his teeth and looked towards the ceiling. How could he explain it to someone like her? Did he even want to?

"What if this isn't all that there is?" His tone was softer, more distant as his mind worked through the concepts, rapidly trying to translate thoughts into words. "What if this place, all of this, what if it's just one of many? What if there are other universes, other dimensions? They wouldn't need to follow our rules, our laws. They would have their own. What if those dimensions were to bleed into ours, what would that look or sound like? Could it sound like a telephone ringing in the dark?"

The doctor closed the book and crossed her hands atop its cover.

"Leo, I understand this is difficult. I'm certain you must feel as if you are losing your grip, but I assure you, you are not. I feel that an MRI is beyond necessary at this point. Leo, we need to understand what is happening inside of you before it is too late."

He clenched his fists. His foot tapped rapidly against the floor.

"I've seen things doctor; I've seen things you wouldn't understand. The stranger, he told me, but I didn't believe him, not until I saw it. The phone, it's not really a phone, it's just... it's an idea, a concept. Something I can understand, something my mind can use to translate." He was shaking now. His foot tapped even faster against the carpet. "I've been taking... vitamins... and the blinding light and pain hasn't come back. I answered the phone doctor! I answered it! I spoke to them!"

Leo took a deep breath and leaned back in the couch. He had been yelling. Doctor Ipsom merely watched on; her expression unchanging.

"And what did they say, Leo?" Her voice was soft, compassionate even.

"I broke something. A door. Or opened it, I don't know. They gave me a... code of some sort, and then a stranger visited me. He wasn't from here; I could tell even before he said anything. I answered the phone again the other night. I saw… colors… and shapes… things I could never explain to anyone… things I hardly understand myself. I saw perfection."

A tear rolled down his cheek. Emotions coursed through him. Part of it was the overwhelming feelings that came from remembering that experience, the other part was extreme sleep deprivation. How many days had it been now? Three? Four? He had lost count. Sleep was a distraction. There was so much more now, so much he had to understand, so much he had to make others understand. How many times had he started over on that painting?

"Leo," the doctor leaned forward, there was sadness in her eyes, "Leo, listen to me. I know you don't like me; I know you never have, but I do care about you. The MRI is not because I think you are crazy; I need you to know that. You are a brilliant mind Leo, a brilliant mind and an incredible artist. I envy the way you see the world. Sometimes, the world we see can be changed and manipulated by our own brains. Things can happen, sicknesses that we have no control over. I just want to make sure that you are not sick, Leo."

He nodded and rose to his feet, buttoning his jacket as he moved towards the door.

"And when you find no tumor what then? You put me on medication? When that doesn't work, then what? You lock me in a padded cell so I don't hurt anyone or myself? Tie me in a straight-jacket until the second-hand ticks down, and I waste away to ash and smoke and float up into the stars? No doctor. With all due respect, I do not trust you. Consider our business arrangement terminated."

With that, he grabbed the door handle and left the room. Everything was red, but red wasn't the right color anymore. No, there was another color somewhere that his eyes couldn't see, somewhere his mind couldn't truly grasp. That was the true color of rage. That non-color that he couldn't quite understand. The idea frustrated him. He had been completely fine with red, but now he had seen something else and red would never cut it again.

"Same time next week Mr. Harr?" Connie's voice rang through his ears. He heard it, but he didn't care. Words flowed from his mouth, words he neither chose nor desired to remember.

"Have a good one, Connie," he muttered as he pushed through the glass doors into the frigid air beyond.

His toe throbbed and ached. He should go to a hospital and get it looked at, but what would they do about a broken toe? Give him medication and tell him to stay off it for a while. No, he would be fine. It was just a toe.

Pulling his jacket tight, he wandered along the sidewalk, down random streets and alleyways, moving through the city like a ghost with no sense of direction or care for where his legs took him. Maybe the doctor was right, maybe he had a tumor. He had done enough drugs in his past to break something inside of his brain. He blinked and saw in the back of his eyelids the inverted triangle unfurling its petals in a rainbow of non-color.

No, he wasn't crazy. He couldn't be. His toe proved that it hadn't been a dream or a hallucination. It had been real, as real, maybe realer than the world around him. The smell of trash filled his nostrils, the sound of a pigeon rattled in his ears. This was all just as real as what he had experienced. There was more than this though, more than all of this.

He watched the people passing by. Eyes locked on cell phone screens, or on the ground, or staring straight ahead like maniacs. Each one of them believed that what they were, who they were, and what they experienced was everything. They believed the color wheel was a map of all colors, that right angles and spheres were the only geometry. Leo passed them one by one and felt more detached from their world than ever before. How could he make them understand? Could he make them understand at all? He shook his head. No, there was no way unless they saw for themselves. And how many of them would see and still choose not to believe?

Reaching into his jacket pocket, Leo retrieved the pack of cigarettes. This was a fresh pack, the fifth he had purchased. He had burned through the rest of them. Pulling a cigarette from the package, he placed it in his lips and lit it. The smoke curled around the glowing tobacco, folding and twisting before it dissipated into the air. He chuckled to himself as he inhaled deeply.

How many universes, just like his own, were contained in that puff of smoke? How many people existed there, each thinking their geometry or colors or sound was the only way it could be? How many shrinks were telling their Leos to go get an MRI because he might have a brain tumor? He shook his head and took another drag off the cigarette. Maybe he was losing his mind, seeing universes in puffs of cigarette smoke.

C Major... Elm... Turquoise Shell...

He remembered the key this time. Three disparate concepts that would come together to prove an identity. It had happened before, and it would happen again. He was certain of it. An image flashed behind his blinking eyelids. A red door. It changed form even as he saw it. At once it was Victorian, Baroque, modern, stained glass. He did not understand what the red door meant, or what it truly was. Nor did he understand why he had to be afraid of it.

Leo turned his head towards the sky and let the sun warm his face. If he was insane, then he never wanted to be anything else. There was something liberating about this insanity, something freeing. He was more than just an artist, more than just a cog in the massive machine of time. He had a purpose, a meaning, a reason.

He chuckled. Who was he kidding? He could lie to himself about purpose and meaning, but in reality, he knew the truth. He was crazier than a run-over cat.

CHAPTER 10

THE LULL

Vehicles drove by, their once-pure surfaces now coated in a hazy sheen of pallid death. Pale horses roaring down the streets, each one laughing and mocking Leo as he stood silent before the convenience store, his skin washed in the red glow of the neon sign. A frigid fog had descended upon the city, a fog that diffused the colors, disintegrating pinpricks of light and scattering them into massive glowing orbs that hung suspended over slick pavement. This long twilight would continue for hours. Hours of half-light and mutated wavelengths.

Leo lowered his head and entered the store, wincing as the bell dinged to mark his arrival. Two shoppers waited in line behind a homeless man, his hair ragged and his clothes disheveled. He smelled like damp fish. A visibly frustrated Joe tried to decipher which pack of cigarettes the man was asking for by pointing to different colored boxes. Each attempt ended with a shake of the head and some nearly inhuman screech of failure from the homeless man.

"Just tell me which one you want dammit!" Joe roared, slamming his hands against the counter.

"A'r d' g'e li' mah'ru!" The homeless man yelled back in a high pitched guttural staccato.

"Dude!" Joe's head rolled back, as he lifted his hands to his face and rubbed his eyes.

"He wants the Marlboro Lights." Leo muttered from the back of the line as he lifted his phone from his pocket to check his messages. He didn't even unlock it; he didn't need to. Dozens of missed calls and texts hung on his lock-screen, most from Lucille, some from unknown numbers. She was worried. He hadn't spoken to her since their date. How long ago had that been now?

"Marlboro Lights? Is that what you want?"

The homeless man replied with a vicious nod. Joe cussed under his breath as he retrieved the pack, muttering to himself the entire way. As soon as the cigarettes hit the counter, the homeless man snatched them up and sprinted out of the store, laughing his way down the sidewalk as the fog swallowed him. Joe didn't yell or holler after the man, he just stared in his direction and shook his head before waving the next customer up.

Leo stared into the fog. He watched the man disappear into it repeatedly in a loop of fractured time. He felt a kindred bond with that man, a friendship of spirit. How close was he to being just like him? Wasting away in a back alley using yesterday's newspaper as toilet paper, muttering about the colors no one else would see?

"Leo?" Joe's voice cut through the haze of sleep deprivation. Leo snapped towards the sound, his sight falling into focus, transforming Joe from a fuzzy black caterpillar into a proper human.

"Hey Joe. Rough day?" Leo nodded back towards the door, but his facial expression never changed.

"Dude," Joe leaned over the counter, looking Leo up and down, "you look like shit."

"Yea," Leo nodded, managing a half-smile, "can I get three more packs? No, four. Actually… just give me the carton."

Joe paused before retrieving the box as if considering whether he would get them at all.

"You went from zero smokes to a pack a day in a week? Dude, you look like shit. I don't know if I told you that. When was the last time you slept?" Joe held the carton in his right hand, not making any effort to ring the product up. It was obvious he wasn't going to let Leo leave without a conversation.

Leo sighed. "Uh… four? I don't know. What day is it?"

"Dude," Joe reached behind him and pulled up a stool. It creaked as he dropped himself onto it, his massive form swallowing it whole. "What's the deal, man?"

This wasn't the place nor the time. Leo liked Joe, respected him even. Hell, he would have gotten a beer with the guy if the opportunity had presented itself. But he didn't want to tell Joe about his personal life. Frankly, it was none of the man's business. But what if Joe believed him? Of anyone, Joe would be the most likely to entertain Leo's wild ideas without passing judgment. No doubt Lucille thought he was insane, and he knew for certain the doctor did. Joe was already his own special kind of broken. Maybe that was just the person he needed to talk to.

"You ever think about other dimensions? What it would be like if you could break into one and peek around?"

"You mean like time travel? Like Star Trek type shit? Where you meet yourself, but it's not you: it's the other version of you if you had done shit different?" Joe was all in, Leo could tell from the look in his eyes.

"No, not like that. Like a place entirely different. A place outside of anything we could understand." The feeling of crazy was peeling away layer by layer as he watched Joe soak in the words, the cogs in his mind turning and turning as he tried to understand.

"Oh, you mean like God or some shit? I thought you were an atheist." Joe chuckled and pulled a half-eaten sandwich from somewhere under the counter.

"I don't know what I believe anymore." Leo shook his head and rubbed his eyes. "I think I'm going crazy. I saw something, something I couldn't even try to explain to you. The shapes, they weren't like ours. Non-Euclidean would be the word to use, but these were different than even that. These made me understand that it's not as simple as Euclidean and Non-Euclidean. There are so many variations and shades of physics, geometry, color, sound, existence itself. It's so much, and it's all real, out there beyond whatever this is."

A dollop of mayo slid out from between the bread and dropped onto Joe's shirt as he took a bite of his sandwich. He didn't bother to clean it up, instead he merely nodded and placed the sandwich back onto the counter.

"I was raised Catholic," Joe started, licking the mayo off his lips, "I never really bought into the whole thing. All that, sit down, stand up, kneel, pray, back up, sit your ass down, hail Mary, stand back up. It all seemed like bullshit to me, even as a kid. I remember sitting in Mass, staring at some image of Jesus or the disciples or some shit, and I remember thinking to myself–I was like ten years old too–I remember thinking, 'why would Jesus look like that?' right?

"Like, this is supposed to be God, the thing, the dude who created everything. Shit man, like we are talking about a dude who they're saying is three fuckin' guys at once right? And here they always make him look the same. And I remember thinking, what would it really look like? Like, to see the face of God or an angel or heaven or whatever. And I remember thinking that the colors would be different. They'd have to be. If there were any colors at all.

"And all the people around me, they're talking about a crystal castle in the sky or whatever and they have it, an image in their mind of what they think it would be like. And I remember thinking if you can picture it then you have to be wrong. It doesn't make any sense otherwise."

A warmth fell upon Leo as the tension in his mind and muscles slid down in between the cracks of the dirty tile floor. Most people would look at Joe, hear him say a few words, and think he was a Grade-A moron. He wasn't though. Instead he was a priest. A priest to the lost and broken whose pulpit was an old milk crate sagging beneath his incredible weight as he preached lines of prophetic importance to the unwashed masses who hung on every one of those words spoken so poetically between insults and sexual innuendo.

"That's just it. I don't even know if I did see anything at all. Could I know? What if it was some vivid dream I've been latching onto this entire time? I mean, how could we comprehend anything that was so... 'other'... when all we know is this? How could someone understand a tree if they'd never seen one before? If they'd only ever lived in a single block of a sprawling city would they picture it like a sparkling streetlight? A resplendent thing that glowed with dozens of iron arms painted green and brown? I feel like I'm crazy, and maybe I am. I don't know anymore."

Joe shook his head. "You have that look in your eyes. I've seen that look before. Saw it on my brother when we found him in the woods back home, back when I was like fifteen or sixteen. He'd been lost for over a week, no one knew where he was. Get this, we fuckin' find him, and he's jabbering about aliens and silver platters flying through the sky. Swears up and down they abducted him. No one believes him. My parents, shit, they sent him right down to the funny farm. Didn't wait a damn second to do it either. The minute the word 'aliens' left my brother's lips they were over it. I remember that look in his eyes when he was telling us. He believed it. He believed that whatever he thought he had seen was real. Shit man, maybe it was. That's the thing, though. No one will ever know but him."

"Do you think he was crazy?" Leo asked, his foot tapping against the floor.

"Nah," Joe shook his head and snatched up the sandwich, "he believed it man. And that's really all that matters, I think. Crazy is that hobo who stole my pack of cigarettes. Fuckers like that never ask themselves if they are crazy, the thought doesn't enter their minds. They think everyone else is crazy. See, that's what makes someone actually crazy, man. It's when you start to believe that all those people around you are the crazy ones. When you start thinkin' you're the last sane one in the room, that's when you need to be locked away.

"My brother, he believed what he saw, but he didn't think anyone else was crazy for doubting him. Hell, he tried to kill himself before they sent him away because he thought his brain was too fucked up to keep going.

"The way I see it, if you think you're crazy, then you're probably fine. Shit man, I wonder if I'm crazy most days myself, and I ain't never experienced anything wild or unnatural. I'm just a dude who runs this shit show you see around you, living a pretty vanilla life. The hardest things I have to work through are what to put on the sandwiches I sell from day to day. I think everyone wonders if they're crazy man, that's just how it goes."

Leo nodded and pulled the wallet from his back pocket, grabbing a bill and sliding it across the counter. A holy silence descended upon that dingy plastic church with its stained-glass windows of advertisement posters and neon signs. He wanted to cry; he wanted to break down and weep in repentance right there on the cracked tile floor, surrounded by Kit-Kats and beef jerky. His eyes turned towards the Technicolor cigarette boxes that surrounded Joe's head like a halo. He wanted to beg Joe to call someone to come haul him away, to take him to the confessional of white padded cells and straight-jackets where he could unburden himself of his sins.

"Here's what you need to do." Joe paused to let out a loud belch as he snatched up a to-go pack of sleeping pills and slapped them on the counter. "You obviously aren't fuckin' sleeping. That's a problem. Sooner or later your body is gonna burn itself out, and then you'll be shit out of luck. These are on the house. Take a few and just sleep. Take a nap. A long one. Like a twenty-four-hour long one."

Leo focused on that portrait of Saint Joe the convenience store clerk, a shower of heavenly glory raining down upon his head, pouring from a flickering fluorescent bulb in the grimy ceiling. The patron saint of cigarettes and sleeping pills, giving communion with cheap beer and potato chips as he baptized your head with a splash of liquor he kept stashed behind the counter.

"I appreciate it." Leo snatched the foil-wrapped pack of salvation from Joe's mayonnaise covered fingers. He turned it over in his hand, his eyes studying the dosage instructions like scripture.

"No sweat. Hey, look. No offense or anything, but I wouldn't go around tellin' too many people that you saw something. Shit, they might haul you up town like they did my brother. Now I'm not saying you're crazy, don't get me wrong, but people aren't very understanding. You challenge their ideas of what is real and they get pretty fuckin' pissed off. Maybe approach it more... what's the word... theoretical." He paused, eyes drifting towards the ceiling as though receiving a message from Heaven itself. "You know what's funny man? People love to think about the unknown. They love it when a Neil deGrasse Tyson talks about wormholes or a Steven Hawking talks about time loops, but you tell em that you've seen or experienced somethin' like that and they lose their damn minds.

"Shit man, you can talk all day in the form of 'what if?' and everyone and their mother gets in on the conversation. The minute you say 'it is' or 'I saw' they grab their pitchforks and torches and get real angry. The thing is man, if it could be, then why can't it be? Like, if you're going to accept the idea that it's possible, then why get so upset if someone says they experienced it? I don't know man. Fuckin' people these days."

So concluded the sermon of Saint Joe.

"How are the veggie burgers coming along?" Leo asked, sliding the wad of change and sleeping pills into his coat pocket as he grabbed the carton of cigarettes.

"It's the same shit, man. People believe what they want to believe and god forbid you believe what you want to believe if it isn't what the fuck they want you to believe."

All rise.

"Isn't that the truth," Leo muttered as he turned back towards the door.

Mass was over, and it was time to leave, time to go back to wherever it was you came from and have a nice cold beer while you watched the Sunday game.

The bell dinged as he exited the bright lights of the store and was swallowed by the suffocating fog and perpetual half-darkness of twilight. Far in the distance a construction sign glowed a vibrant orange as its bulbs flicked between messages. Leo couldn't read the sign, to him it was just a massive blob of neon. He didn't have to read it though; he understood it as it was. Someone had placed it there just for him. Perhaps Saint Joe had come down and dropped it there, perhaps it had been the stranger who entered his house. Either way, the globe of light said plenty without words.

"Be careful. And watch your step."

CHAPTER 11

THE OFFER

Leo stared at his half-finished painting through the haze of cigarette-smoke. An inverted triangle of blacks and purples rotated towards him in an overly reflective tunnel of kaleidoscope rainbows. It wasn't right though. It was a mockery of the real thing, a parody of beauty itself. It was, for lack of a better word, pathetic.

Another cloud of blue-gray smoke billowed across his vision, obscuring the painting even further. It almost looked better this way, half-visible, smoke curling around its edges. Something about the movement gave it weight and possibility. Without the smoke it might as well have been a child's attempt at art.

Leaning his head back against the couch, he stared towards the ceiling. He closed his eyes and took a long drag off the cigarette. His body felt calmer now, his mind clearer. He felt like he could breathe again. He took a deep breath and broke into a coughing fit as the tar detached from the walls of his lungs. Phlegm and mucus mixed with saliva as he coughed the tar into the rag he had used to clean his brushes. A tear rolled down his face from the strain, he smiled. This physical difficulty was preferable to that terrible feeling that someone was standing on his chest. Anything was better than feeling that the tension in your muscles was slowly crushing you to death.

The sleeping pills had worked, he had finally slept, and his sleep, for once in such a long time, had been dreamless. A perfect void of nothing that his body coasted along for the blink of an eye before waking hours later. It had been heaven.

The cigarette sizzled and popped as he pressed it into the ashtray, forcing it to fit between the dozens of butts already crammed into that small dish. For a moment he imagined them as men in business suits aboard New York public transit, all packed in together, shoulder to shoulder, pressed against each other as they made their ways to the same tin-can buildings to work the same cookie-cutter jobs and go home to the same one-bedroom apartments.

He smiled and pulled another cigarette from the pack and lit it. At least he wasn't one of them. That smile faded as his eyes fell back upon that half-finished painting.

He wanted to feel rage at the inadequacies of his talents, but he couldn't grab hold of it. There was only deep sorrow, a sorrow that he might never see that eternal beauty ever again.

He had never tried heroin, though he knew plenty of people who had. His friend Marcus had described that first high as something so perfect, so incredible that all he had ever wanted to do was find it again. 'Chasing the dragon' people called it, and that dragon was all Marcus used to think about, even when he wasn't high. It was his everything.

Had been.

Until the day he overdosed, his body found by his girlfriend, cold and hard like a statue leaned up against the wall of his tiny apartment surrounded by used syringes and Pedialyte. She described him as having a smile on his face, a placid smile of contentment. Leo liked to think that Marcus had found that original perfect, that maybe, instead of coming back and dealing with the misery of losing it again, he had decided to stay there forever. If given the choice, Leo would have done the same. This was his dragon, that inverted triangle that mocked him from the canvas.

A sound chirped from the door, followed by another and another. A rapid succession of beeps echoing from the security pad. Leo jumped to his feet, cigarette still in hand, and rushed towards the screen. Lucille stood in full view; her eyes focused on the camera. For a moment Leo stood frozen, terror gripping his chest. Gone was the playful sexuality or even that veiled intensity. In its place was rage, pure and unadulterated rage. Lucille was furious.

Without a word, he buzzed her in. His foot tapped nervously against the floor as he stared at the door, waiting, counting down the seconds.

She knocked at the door, and he answered. Silently she glided by him, waving away the cigarette smoke that curled and danced around her head. Leo peeked into the hallway, watching for anyone who may have followed her up. His paranoia was growing. He had this incredible feeling that someone was watching him, someone who shouldn't be watching him, someone he didn't want watching him. Shutting and locking the door, he turned back, drawing in another lung-full of smoke.

"So, this is it then?" Lucille's eyes studied the empty boxes of cigarettes strewn throughout the apartment before turning towards Leo and planting her hands on her hips.

"What?" He shrugged as if he didn't care, though inside he was a ball of anxiety.

"You've ghosted me for a week, and that's all you have to say? I thought you quit smoking?" Her tone modulated between violently angry and exceedingly concerned.

"I didn't mean to. I mean… Look, I'm all kinds of fucked up right now. I didn't mean to make you worry. To be honest, I didn't even realize how many days it had been." He moved back towards the couch and slumped into it, swapping his finished cigarette with a fresh one.

"You're chain-smoking now?"

"I guess. Yea. I didn't even realize."

Lucille sighed and glided towards the windows, un-latching and opening them one by one. The fog and haze cleared as the fresh air swapped places with its filthy counterpart. Leo studied the churning cloud as it billowed out into the city. He wondered if someone looking up from below might worry there had been a fire.

"What's going on Leo?" She stood in front of the couch; arms crossed. Anger rippled across her face, but in her voice all Leo could hear was worry.

"I hadn't been sleeping. I think it was something like four days, maybe more? What day is it? Doesn't matter. I had to take sleeping pills last night but I finally got some sleep. I've just been trying to get my shit together since. Yesterday I saw all your missed calls, and I meant to call you back, I just... man I was so tired. I'm sorry Lucille, I really am. I don't know what's wrong with me lately."

He put the cigarette down and turned his full attention towards her. She was incredible, a masterpiece. How could he have made her worry? He should have been better to her, he needed to be better to her. She was a shard of heaven itself, a glass fragment of perfection he had been tasked with protecting. What would he ever do if that glass shattered?

"You aren't lying, are you?" She unfolded her arms and took a seat on the far side of the couch. Her eyes never left his.

"No," he muttered, shaking his head, "no, I'm not lying."

"Is this about the stuff you told me at dinner the other day?"

"Yes."

What had he told her? How long ago had it been? It felt like months, but had it only been a few days? He opened his mouth to say more, but the words weren't there. There was nothing much to say. He could keep apologizing, but that wouldn't make anything better. Not really. Instead, he closed his mouth and allowed the silence to descend upon the room.

She sighed and turned her attention towards the painting. A wave of embarrassment crashed down upon him as he looked up towards that hideous thing. Blasphemous was the only word to describe it. This monstrosity was not fit for viewing, not by anyone, especially not by Lucille.

"What's this?" She asked, cocking her head to the side as she tried to understand it.

"It's nothing. Just some bullshit I was trying. It's bad. I hate it." He more than hated it. He despised it. Its very existence was repulsive. It needed to be burned, and the tools and paints he used to make it needed to be burned, and the hands that wielded those tools needed to be burned, and the mind that conceived it needed to be burned. All the way until his very soul was tossed into a cosmic trash compactor and spit out the other side of a supernova.

"It's… it's absolutely beautiful." The sincerity in her voice made him taste bile. He struggled not to vomit.

Suddenly her entire appearance morphed before him and Aphrodite transformed into Medusa. What kind of person could look upon this blasphemous work and think it was beautiful? He shook his head and pressed his fingers into his eyes. No, to her it might be. She had never seen the real the thing.

"Leo, what's the matter?" He felt her soft touch against his arms as she pulled his hands from his face. He opened his eyes and for a moment thought he was seeing the face of an angel. She smiled at him, and the pain went away.

"It's just... it's not what I wanted it to be. I'm frustrated. I have this... idea in my head... and I can't make it happen on canvas."

She stared at him with that understanding that only a fellow artist could have. It was the curse of the creative mind, to watch forever as you destroyed perfect ideas with your own hands. No words, no paints, no shapes, no colors existed to create that which exists inside of a mind, not truly, not the way you imagine it. No matter how hard you try you always look at what you've made and think, 'burn it, burn it all.' Lucille understood that. It made him feel better to know that someone did.

"Leo, I've never seen you like this. Have you talked to your therapist about it?"

Leo laughed out loud, "Oh yea. She's not my therapist anymore. She thinks I'm insane. Wanted me to get that MRI so when it came back negative she could have them lock me away somewhere, or drug me up on god only knows what until my brain burnt out. Yea, I talked to her about it. I would say it didn't go very well."

Her hands fell away, and she recoiled. He could see it in her eyes, the worry that maybe he was, in fact, going insane. Part of him wanted to do everything he could to convince her that wasn't the case, but then he looked back towards the painting and instantly revulsion and disgust filled him, drowning out all other thought and emotion. He wanted to jump off the couch and tear the canvas to shreds. He had to force himself to remain seated. It was then he realized he was grinding his teeth.

"Leo, I want to help you, but I don't know how."

A tear rolled down her face and his heart shattered into a million tiny pieces, each one flaying his soul in a thousand places. Watching an angel cry was, in itself, a sorrowful weight, but knowing you had caused it was enough to break you down and crush your spirit into dust.

"Lucille–" he started; voice soft as he reached towards her. She shook her head.

"Leo. I want you to come stay with me. I have plenty of room, and… oh, I don't know. Maybe having someone around will help you. I… I can't watch you do this to yourself." She wiped the tear away and closed her eyes, taking a deep breath. In an instant she was composed, almost no hint of that internal fracture remained. "You said something about strange pills at dinner, are you still taking those?"

Leo's eyes darted towards the counter where the translucent bottle of unmarked pills sat. He nodded.

"Yea, every day like the guy told me to."

"Do you think that maybe that's the problem? Maybe these strange drugs you're taking are messing with your head?" Her eyes pierced his and for a moment there was nothing, no sound, no smell, no touch, just two souls existing in a place outside of time itself. For a moment Leo thought he could see those colors again, those incredible non-colors of eternity dancing in her hazel eyes.

"It could be. I don't know. I have this... feeling... that he wasn't lying. That I have to do what he said, that I have to fix what I broke." It was more than a feeling; it was a memory. His own memory staring back at him in mockery from the canvas.

"Leo," she reached towards him and clasped his hands in hers, "you didn't break anything. There's nothing to fix. I need you Leo, I need you to be well. I'll help you however I can. I promise."

She slid towards him and placed her head against his chest. Her hair smelled like roses. He closed his eyes and held her close. He wanted to shatter. He wanted his heart to break through whatever wall existed between them and melt into hers. Instead, he turned and stared at that taunting triangle. Even as he caressed her back and held his Aphrodite close, all he could think about was that elusive dragon.

CHAPTER 12

THE PARK

Leo rested his hands in his lap as his eyes watched the clouds float across the vast ocean of sky. Branches that would, in just a few short months, obscure this view with fresh life hung leafless overhead like crippled fingers. An echo of Mozart's Symphony No. 41 danced on the wind from somewhere far in the distance, so faint, that Leo wondered for a moment if it was only in his mind.

This small park was a place of solitude. A place for contemplation. He brought no cigarettes here. To do so would be a blasphemous assault on this tranquil sanctuary. Instead, he merely sat and existed as nature moved around him, thriving without a care for the pain of those who trudged across its hallowed ground. It had no care for his problems or concerns, or those of anyone else. It simply was. In this place there was only one reality, and that reality was crafted of chlorophyll and carbon.

He wanted to weep; he wanted to break down and cry right there on that park bench. The weight of everything was too great. How long could he hold on? How long could he maintain a semblance of normalcy until finally, at some point in an indeterminate future, he cracked and shattered like a porcelain vase, his mind and soul sprinkling upon the carpet as his body fell limp from the chair, the .45 slamming into the floor like a period as that final explosion, that final cry for help still rang out, screaming across eternities, proclaiming to all who would hear that Leo Harr had lived, and now he lived no longer. He shuddered at the thought as he stood over his still twitching corpse, watching it melt into the floor along with all his hopes and dreams and every painting he'd ever made, and all his money and wealth and fame, now gone, running into the cracks in the floorboards, dripping down into the apartment below.

The symphony was reaching its crescendo, the sound writhing through the streets until it landed in this park, transforming those few remaining brown leaves into ballerinas of sound that danced and fluttered about him. For a moment he saw this place– this small patch of forest amidst a thriving city–the way he had seen that inverted triangle of impossible colors. This place was equally beautiful, equally stunning, and equally awe-inspiring. The colors, sounds, and shapes might not be new and foreign, but together they formed their own spiritual picture of perfection. There was beauty for him here, he had not lost it in that other place after all.

A young girl rounded the corner, walking along the path alone, carrying in her hand a balloon tethered by a white string. The smell of ozone filled his nostrils. That moment of beauty shattered as his eyes beheld the balloon's shape. A turtle with a turquoise shell. His breathing stopped as he realized the surrounding trees, almost all of them, were elms. The small girl, no older than ten, walked up to the bench and took a seat next to him. Leo closed his eyes. He knew who this was. The plainness of her features had not been immediately apparent, but now that he had noticed them, he could never un-see them. It was like looking at every young child mashed together, boys and girls alike, their features amalgamated into a sick average that was so plain that it might as well be a new creature altogether.

"Hello Leo." Her voice could have belonged to any child, it was so plain, too plain. A chill ran down his spine. "We hope you are doing well."

Leo clenched his jaw as his foot began tapping against the ground. He wanted out of this whole endeavor. He wanted his life back. No, it was more than that. He wanted his mind back.

"What do you want?" He spoke without looking, instead focusing his eyes back towards the heavens and the pools of blue sky that gathered between the banks of the white clouds.

"Has anyone given you anything to hold on to?" It sounded so strange coming from a child. The words themselves so innocent and naïve, though Leo knew the thing sitting next to him was neither.

"No," he snapped, "why do you keep asking me that?"

"What you view as a scrap of paper, a briefcase, or even a book, could be much more Leo. The Unraveled could hand you something that seems innocent and harmless, yet it could be a Double Meaning, transmitting data through the Break. We must take all precautions."

Leo chuckled, "So what about these trees? They could be listening too right?"

"Impossible. Organic material, especially that of the Double Helix cannot be a vessel for the Double Meaning. This must seem like a contradiction, since you are currently seeing me in the form of an organic creation. However, these Reality Boxes we wear are merely vessels. They seem human, but they are not formed of the Double Helix. This is more complicated than you understand, would you like us to explain further? We will if it helps you." The face of an innocent girl stared at him expectantly, awaiting a reply as the balloon danced on the breeze above her head. Leo shifted uncomfortably. He didn't like this form one bit. He preferred the older bald man; it was much less unnerving.

"No, that's okay. Hey, next time can you not come looking like... this? It's... disconcerting. I liked the other guy better."

The girl nodded. "We can accommodate such a request."

Leo sighed, he suddenly felt exhausted. The color and beauty melted from the scene around him, leaving nothing but shades of brown and gray in their place. A sorrow threatened to wash over him. He wanted to be free; he wanted be done with this insanity.

That's what it was, insanity. He was insane. Talking to children on park benches as if they were from other dimensions. How must that look to someone passing by? No, he couldn't simply toss it all aside as something so simple, there was something going on here. Unless the child was a figment of his imagination. Perhaps the bald man had been too. An image of the inverted triangle appeared in his mind's eye. He knew he wasn't making any of this up. It was unfortunate. He wished he was.

"Did the medication cure the effects of the Afterbleed?"

"Yes, I think. I don't know. Were you the triangle? What was all that? What did I see?" Answers, he needed answers. This thing next to him, it might have them. He wanted to grab hold of that child and shake her until she said something that made him feel human again, that might give him back some part of his mind that he lost along the way. Instead, he sat still, eyes focused straight ahead. He dared not look at her.

"No, we are not what you understood to be a triangle. You saw the limits of what your being can process. You and your kind, your entire reality is a paradox, limited by the constraints of the Double Helix. However, inside– beyond your internal Break so to speak–there is another, or rather, there is the One. Some would call this the soul, others might call it the state of being, there is no word to express it in your language, nor one your Double Helix mind can grasp. What you experienced, you experienced not with your mind or your body, but with the One. Your kind have the capacity to understand far beyond the limits of the Double Helix, however it is exceedingly difficult and can cause… problems."

Leo paused. Something about those words made sense. Why did they have to make sense? "So, did I see God or something?"

The girl chuckled, he could see her shaking her head out of the corner of his eye. "No. You stood at the threshold of a higher reality that exists above your own. You stood at the edge of the Break and stared into the Other. There are Others that are higher still and Others that are lower. There are some high enough that even we cannot comprehend their Otherness. That disorientation you felt is what we feel when we travel here into the Transit, or when we travel down too low, or up too high. You must understand that the Others do not touch, save for where they touch the Transit. We believe your reality's paradox is what ties them to this place, and we are certain that same paradox is what allows us to use this as a conduit for our travel, though doing so causes great distress and disorientation. This is why we have created these Reality

Boxes, to lessen the effects of the Otherness so we may pass through more comfortably."

Leo sniffled and wrinkled his nose. The smell of ozone was growing stronger, though he wasn't certain why.

"I haven't been sleeping. Not since I started taking those pills. What are they doing to me? Why can't I sleep anymore?" His voice did not ask, it demanded.

The girl turned and stared at him for a moment. He felt her eyes studying him, but he refused to look.

"The medication does not interfere with your physiology in any way. It does nothing to your Double Helix structures. It is to treat the One inside of you, that which forms the paradox. There are no side effects."

"So, you're saying this is a spiritual medicine? That this pill I pop in my mouth and swallow is for my soul?" He wanted to laugh, he wanted to get up and walk away from the madness, but he couldn't. The ideas were so foreign and strange, the concepts so vague, that he felt the need to hear them out.

It reminded him of the time he had spent an evening with a homeless man in Atlanta who called himself Napoleon. The man swore up and down he was the reincarnation of the famous French Emperor. Leo didn't believe him, but it made for an interesting evening and he had been curious where it would go. By the end of the night Leo had found himself wondering if reincarnation was truly a thing, and if just possibly, the French Emperor had been sent back into the body of a one-eyed homeless man in Georgia.

"In a sense, yes. It is to reduce the damaging effects that experiencing things beyond the Break can have upon your paradox. That Otherness that you experience, that discomfort and jarring disorientation of the Afterbleed begins in the One. We believe that the One has a desire to remain in the Other, where it feels more at home and comfortable, however it is bound to the Double Helix and so must return to the Transit.

"The Afterbleed is a resulting effect of the struggle between your internal paradox. The medication helps strengthen the bond between the Double Helix you and the internal, Other you, thus eliminating the discomfort of travel. It is imperative that you do not stop taking them, else we cannot contact you so easily. Without the medication the signals will be disrupted as your internal paradox struggles to separate from itself. Were this to continue, the long-term damage would be catastrophic. Your paradox would split in two, and you, your two yous, would wander separate planes, belonging to neither."

The words sounded ridiculous coming from the mouth of a ten-year-old girl, yet after his prior experience he understood exactly what those words meant. A husk devoid of a soul, and a soul devoid of a body, both existing simultaneously, both him, yet neither fully him, and neither fully existing. The very idea of such an existence reminded him of the biblical descriptions of Hell.

"So why are you here? I'm sure you didn't come to answer my questions." Leo swallowed hard. It all made too much sense, but even that sense of understanding did little to lessen the feeling of insanity that coursed through him, in fact it did the opposite. Each time he understood those nonsense words spoken by a ten-year-old, it seemed to confirm his greatest fears.

"This Reality Box is stronger than the last. We may remain longer than before. Answering your questions is important. You must understand in order to fix what you have broken. However, you are correct. We did not come just to answer your questions, though we knew they would be many. We have learned more about the door. It is not broken. We all are very thankful for this.

"The door, rather than being broken, is ajar. Instead of repairing it, you must close it. This is a simpler task than repairing a hole, however it is still not an easy one. The Underlower is far below, too far for us to see it clearly. We understand its general location, but much like you had difficulty standing at the edge of our Other, so we have the same difficulty standing at the edge of theirs. In addition, they mean us harm, whereas we welcomed you. Standing at the edge of an Other is a strange experience even for those such as us.

"The Unraveled inside that Other, they can see us, though we cannot see them, and so they may be able to reach across the threshold and into the Break. We must be careful this does not happen."

The girl paused, her eyes studying Leo's reaction. He licked his lips and swallowed hard. The feeling of crazy tickling the edge of his mind.

"We fear there has been a misunderstanding regarding the red door. We now understand there to be two. One exists here in the Transit, though it is but an icon, a symbol of the Other red door. We do not believe this icon to be any more dangerous than the rest of the Transit, however, there may be Unraveled gathered around this icon. This icon may be used to distract you, but it is not the door you seek. The Other red door, the real red door, that is the one you have opened. That door is exceedingly dangerous, and it is imperative it be closed."

The girl fell silent. A gust of wind knocked the balloon into a nearby branch. It exploded with a loud pop as shards of nylon rained down on them both.

"So where is it then?" Leo asked, expecting more than she had given him. He felt like this creature was going in circles, giving him enough information to keep him interested while not saying anything in particular.

"The red door is beyond the Break, on the edge of the Underlower, past the threshold. We would take you there, but it is not that simple. To close it, we understand that you must find this place on your own. That is part of the ritual."

"And how do I do that?" Leo folded his arms and turned towards the girl.

"We do not yet know." She jumped down from the bench. "Be careful Leo Harr. Many things may not be what they seem." With that she turned and headed back the way she had come, disappearing into the trees along with that acrid smell of an electrical fire.

Leo closed his eyes, his foot tapping rapidly against the ground. Once again, he was left with more questions than answers, once again he was left feeling like his mind was crumbling into a thousand pieces. A smile crept across his face and he laughed. It was quiet at first, a soft clicking against the roof of his mouth that turned manic as he screamed towards the sky, tears running down his face. Somewhere in the distance Symphony No. 41 ended, replaced by the laughter of a madman that echoed hauntingly through the city.

CHAPTER 13

THE NOTHING//THE NEVER

Leo's keys rattled against his apartment door as he struggled to find the right one. His mind was a blur, a swirling vortex of chaos that trapped and enveloped him, holding him in place as dark thoughts of madness and impending doom beat down upon his psyche. They, someone, something, was after him. He had noticed them on his walk back, people watching him too closely, pretending they weren't watching him at all. He saw the stares, the eyes, the look of familiarity. How many had he counted? Ten, twenty? Had they followed him here?

His head swiveled from side to side, his eyes scanning the hallway for interlopers. The key grabbed and stuck in the lock. He tried to force it, but it wouldn't budge. He slammed his hand against the door in frustration. It was the wrong key.

Heart rate accelerating, he felt the sweat pooling under his arms and running down his forehead as it dripped onto the floor below. Time stopped as he watched the first bead of sweat fall. A black tar-like substance that oozed from his pores like so much blood. Time snapped back into place and the now-clear drop continued its fall, splattering bits of itself against his shoe.

The next key slid in properly, and the lock snapped open with a click. His moist and shaking hands fumbled with the doorknob until finally, after what felt like hours, he found himself on the other side of that door, inside of his own apartment, leaning against it in case someone rushed from behind him and tried to slide their way in. He locked the door and closed his eyes, slowly sliding down its face until he was sitting upon the floor, back hunched, head in his hands, weeping for his lost sanity, or was he weeping for having found it?

It made no difference, really. He was not the Leo he had been a week before. He was something else now. Something entirely… Other. The idea made his skin crawl. No longer could he simply blend in, engaging on a surface level with those around him. No, he knew more than them; he had seen more than them; he was more than them now.

A creak echoed from the hallway outside his apartment, and his chest tightened. He held his breath. He could hear the blood moving in his ears as he strained and struggled to hear what caused that sound. After several moments, he relaxed. Must have just been the building settling.

He lifted his hands to his face, turning them over and over. He hardly recognized them. They were pale, shaking, and glistening with sweat. This paranoia was debilitating. Where had it come from? Had he always been like this? No, there had been a time, not long ago, before the inverted triangle, before the bald man and the little girl, before the pills and the ringing telephone where he had been a laid-back guy. People used to say nothing bothered him, that everything just rolled off his back. Would they even recognize him now?

Then the idea settled upon him. Was he being followed at all? Had those looks been misinterpreted, maybe projections of his paranoia? Had they been normal, everyday people who were just minding their own business whom he had projected his fear upon, contorting them into monsters? Fear had permeated him, soaked into his mind, his soul, it was a part of him now. A part he couldn't seem to carve out.

What did he fear most? Was it the idea of being followed, of being watched, of being tracked and hunted? Or did he fear the bald man and the little girl and what they represented? They knew where he lived. Perhaps these Unraveled they spoke of did not. Even so, there had been no threat of danger, not from the man or the girl, or from any other vague and invisible force that those two so confidently believed were coming for him. Was he afraid of himself? Maybe the man and girl were agents, federal agents. Maybe they knew about his drug habits and his indiscretions of selling a bit on the side. Maybe the feds were after him.

Suddenly, the creaking of the building became the thumping of helicopter blades and the birds outside his window transformed into Blackhawk helicopters, slowly descending as masked men with assault rifles fixed green lasers upon his forehead. He closed his eyes and rocked back and forth. Not real, it wasn't real; he told himself. When he finally opened his eyes again, it was nighttime. Then he remembered it had been nighttime all along. There had never been birds outside his window in the first place.

Leo turned his head towards the counter. In the faint twilight glow, he could barely make out that translucent orange pill bottle. Lucille's voice rang through his head, telling him to stop taking them, telling him that he didn't know what was in them. She was right. They could be poison, they could be low dose psychedelics that were slowly causing his mind to shatter, they could be sugar pills. He had no clue, and yet he had been taking them on pure faith. Based on what? Nothing really. Nothing at all. Perhaps a simple desire to believe was all it had been. Maybe that's all it still was.

The image of the inverted triangle flashed before his eyes, shining in all its impossible glory. For a moment the fear dissipated and in its place emerged that feeling of incredible elation and vitality that had filled him as he stood in that impossible corridor, staring into the rainbow void of eternity itself. No, it was not a desire to believe. It was faith itself. There was something. Something to all of it. There had to be. If there wasn't, then there was no hope left for him.

Leo rose and moved towards the counter. The voice of the little girl, or whatever she had been, echoed in his mind. 'Don't stop taking them, or we cannot contact you.' He had to see that wonder again, somehow. They, or she or, them, or these "Others" wanted him to close a door, but he didn't care about a door, or even if reality itself unwound around him. He merely wanted to stare back into that perfection and allow himself to feel as small as he had the first time.

He reached down and grabbed the bottle and without looking uncapped it, snatched a pill and tossed it into his mouth, swallowing it down dry. Taking a few steps to the side, he fell into his bed, eyes staring at the ceiling as he ran through the events of the past week over and over in his mind. Who was he anymore? Was he still Leo Harr? Of course, he was. Somewhere inside of him was the man he had always been. But there was something else now, too. A layer of too-sane wrapped tight around that old Leo like saran wrap. Soon the old Leo would suffocate to death, or starve, one or the other. And then who would he be? A new Leo? A saner Leo? Would he get a new name? Maybe a new life, a new reality of his own?

Leo shook his head and lifted his hands to his eyes, pressing down with his fingers until the colors and pain blended into a single feeling, a single emotion that washed away the past and the future, leaving him only with the now, the pain, and the color. He screamed and let his arms fall beside him. Everything was upside down. His life, his mind, his emotions.

Opening his eyes, he focused on the gray ceiling, awash in an orange glow from the streetlights outside. The orange swirled, twisting like a vortex, pulling him forward, out of his bed. The wind whipped around him as he dove headfirst into the ceiling. The orange engulfed him, passing over his skin with a vibrant warmth. Were they calling him back? But there had been no ringing phone. There was always a ringing phone, that much never changed.

Suddenly everything stopped. For the briefest moment all was still as time itself froze solid. Leo felt that telltale tightness in his chest and heard that piercing ringing in his ears. Panic welled up inside of him as he realized what was happening. Those pills. They hadn't been the same pills as before. The shape had been different, rounder, not as oval. They had tasted like metal and felt sandy against his teeth. No, he knew what was about to happen. This was the start of a bad trip. A very strong and very terrible trip.

The orange inverted upon itself, that warm glow suddenly malicious and snarling like some ephemeral maw. It thrust him back into his bed, propelling him down with incredible weight, crushing his flesh into a liquid that it squeezed between the fibers of the sheets, then the mattress, then the floorboards themselves. He oozed through it all, screaming without a voice as he was unmade and remade a thousand times in a second. He could feel his soul being extruded through his ears, his mouth, and even his anus. There was nothing he could do; he was powerless here.

The last drop of his body slid through the floorboards and he fell, recombining to form a mutated form of himself that tumbled head over heels through a perfect blackness. All around him red doors opened and closed, slamming shut, rattling, laughing in unspoken languages of malice. Within those doors he could see eyes, strange eyes, octagonal and hexagonal eyes. The colors. He knew those colors. They were not colors from his reality; they were colors from somewhere else. Yet unlike that triangle, these colors were darker, blacker than black, less than nothing, devoid of all and yet full of something he could not, nor did he dare try, to understand.

Evil. This place, this darkness, these things, were evil. Not the evil like from a horror movie, not the kind of evil you could put a name to, or explain to someone else, no this evil was something else. A perfect lack of all that was or ever had been good.

With incredible pain, he slammed against something hard. A black surface, perfectly smooth, wet with something sticky. An inaudible hum permeated his very being, echoing all around him, vibrating through him, pulsating within him. Leo rose to his feet and looked up. Except up was down, and his feet were above him. It made him want to vomit.

He stared forward into the perfect void. No colors existed here, no sounds, no shapes, nothing save for the floor above him. That vibration, that unsound echoed on and on, never stopping, never ceasing, never waning. He couldn't hear it. It wasn't there. Yet it was, and it was everything.

A deep growl reverberated towards him out of the black, the sound of a large stone slab sliding open, or the sound of a snarling wolf readying itself for a kill. The emptiness opened before him, rotating into view. Not a triangle, not even a shape. An emotion. It unfurled before him. Hatred. This was the shape; this was the sound. The void was perfect, haunting, hopeless. He could see the nothing, but only as shades of void. There was less than nothing here, everything was built in shades of nonexistence.

Leo clenched his jaw and ground his teeth as that emotion unfurled its snarling jaws and opened wide to receive him. In its center appeared something, invisible for a moment, yet clear the next. A red door. Bare, devoid of ornamentation, it hung in the nothingness, slightly ajar. It beckoned him closer, but he could not move. A wind rushed around him, moving from behind him towards the door, sucking in the floor, the ooze, the shades of nonexistence and nothingness, devouring it all. He watched his arms and his legs and his chest and his face peel away from his soul as they were sucked inside that door, and then without warning he stood on the other side of it, his back to it, facing three black figures that seemed to be carved from pure obsidian.

They moved, though they never moved. They spoke, though their words were in the spaces between existence in those milliseconds where nothing exists.

"Leo Harr," they said. The malice audible, palpable, tangible.

"We thank you." Their words seemed to take from him, each word seemed to remove a piece of himself, as if instead of imparting information they were stealing it from him and using that blank space to communicate.

"What... why? Who are you? Where am I?" Leo's voice was deafening. The presence of something in this nothing shook it to its very foundations, threatening to demolish it from the inside out. The creatures blinked without eyes and winced without faces. They felt it, he could see they felt it, though he could not see them at all.

"You did us a great service. The Finality approaches."

Leo could feel each atom inside of himself rattle and vibrate, each DNA strand struggling and quivering as it threatened to unravel into spools of goo.

"Finality?" Leo whispered, yet again the world around him shook. Everything sheered in half, the darkness splitting from itself, sliding away from a darker darkness that lay beneath. A facade. This entire thing was a facade. The existence of anything in this place was a ruse, a lie. There was nothing here. He struggled to remember that triangle, but the memory was gone. Everything was that blackness behind the dark, the void behind the nothing, the endlessness of cold hard death he had seen behind this thin veil of unreality itself.

"For your service we may spare you. It is your choice. We have been looking for you, Leo Harr. We have been seeking you out. We have been following you, watching you, waiting for you. You have finally come, but you cannot stay. When the Finality is complete, we will grant you a choice. Until then, go forth and remember. Remember this and remember our power. When next you speak to those above, tell them of us. Tell them of this. Tell them we too can reach you."

With that Leo felt himself pulled backwards through the door, his body sliding through un-space and un-time, through nothingness incarnate as the malice before him furled back in upon itself, swallowing the door, and pulling away into an invisible non-space of perfect blackness. Once more Leo stood before nothing, the floor above him, his head below.

And then he fell.

CHAPTER 14

THE FLATLINE

Leo fell through a gray-scale of blacker blacks, each varying in degrees of intensity. Patches of vibrant darkness pocked with patches of lesser nothingness, creating kaleidoscope images of swirling voids, pits, and caves, each of them sucking in the light and letting none of it escape. Beyond that darkness there were eyes, malicious eyes. Hexagonal, hyperboloid, they rotated and twisted in upon themselves as they gazed at him, hungry, craving to feast upon what little light remained.

He wanted to feel fear, but there was no fear here. There was no joy, no sorrow, no shame, nothing. This place was the absence of everything. He felt his body disintegrating as it fell, like a block of ash falling from a rooftop.

Soon he would be nothing at all. Spread upon this void non-wind, a part of that hideous nothing that surrounded him.

"3, 2, 1, clear."

The words came from everywhere, and nowhere. Time stopped. The rotating void paused and then shattered.

With incredible force Leo felt his body launched out from the sun, the blinding light scorching his eyes and flesh as he hurdled towards earth, passing the planets, satellites, and the moon; burning up in the atmosphere and shredding through ten stories of solid steel before slamming into his own body.

His eyes snapped open. Everything was a blinding white. There were beeps and screeches and strange blue people with no faces staring back at him. A symbol appeared on each of their foreheads. Two teardrops facing each other, divided by the writhing void of a serpent that bent in on itself as it wrapped around those teardrops for all eternity. He recognized that symbol. Infinity.

The symbols on their foreheads grew, and then consumed him, and once more he was falling, surrounded by nothing, if nothing could be less than itself, if nothing had no name, no concept, no idea with which to even describe that it could be, let alone was. This was a complete and total nothing, something so devoid of all and anything that it was alive, and suddenly he was not falling, he was being swallowed by it.

"Clear."

The words paused time once more. He saw those hideous eyes behind the void; he saw the hatred in them as the time slowed and then reversed. He watched as their obsidian claws reached out to hold him down, but they were too slow.

In an instant time had restarted, but backwards, and now he wasn't falling but flying. Rising at light-speed as the void became nothing, then slowly morphed into something, and that something became a house, and that house had walls and a door, and then those doors and walls fell away behind him as the house became a mansion, and so on until he was staring at the underside of a hospital bed, his body forced through it, extruded through the fibers until he was once again staring through his own eyes, back at those hideous blue faceless people who he realized weren't faceless at all. They were doctors and nurses. So many of them. What were they all doing there?

A doctor leaned over the bed and examined him, shining a bright light into his eyes as somewhere close a rhythmic beeping echoed out from a machine. Leo stared into that light. He watched it flex and waver. He watched the strands of infinite color descend from the bulb as they dug into his skin, poking and prodding for a way inside of him. And then they found one. And they peeled him open. He watched all this as his chest broke into a thousand pieces, erupting like Mount St. Helens, spraying the doctors and nurses with gore and blood and violence as the fibers of the light smiled and descended even further; first into his chest and then into his abdomen.

Then it all started again. That light inverted upon itself. The colors became voids of hideous black that stretched across the room, peeling away all life and leaving nothing behind except varying shades of itself. Leo stood in that void, standing atop a checkerboard pattern, three squares by three squares large, each square white, then black, then white again. He stood in its center. He wasn't himself. No, he was a horse. A horse's head to be specific. A horse's head made of wood. A chess piece. A knight. He looked through those wooden eyes at the surrounding board. Panic struck, panic unlike anything that he had ever experienced in his entire life. There weren't enough spaces. He couldn't move.

"Clear."

This time he snapped up from the bed, the blinding light tearing his eyes from his skull, burning away his skin and flesh, peeling the darkness from within him and remaking him anew as he leaned over and vomited onto the floor. He trembled as he wiped the sick from his mouth; he felt the weakness in his bones.

Without a word, he turned his head back towards the doctor. For a moment he saw that writhing serpent on the doctor's forehead, that serpent devouring itself as it sank into the nothing. Yet in a blink it was gone, and Leo collapsed into the bed and everything went dark, but this time, it was his own dark, a dark of colors and tranquil waters, and a rowboat. He was calm, and he was safe.

"Leo?" The words came from an angel. They came from far away, from a world beyond this one, from a place beyond the hospital bed and the beeping sound of his own heart rate. Leo looked up from the rowboat, staring back at the placid glassy waters above, and with a swift motion, he stood and exited the boat.

The sterile lights of the hospital room hurt, not with a burn, but an ache. A dull throbbing pain that he blinked off after a few seconds and thought nothing more of afterward. A blurred shape hung above him, occluding the light. It moved and wavered and then came into focus. It was indeed an angel, the angel herself.

"Lucille." His voice was weak, raspy, shaking. He felt like he could swallow the entire ocean and still need more liquid. How had he gotten here? He could remember pieces, but they were jumbled, mixed up, as if time had ceased to move in a linear pattern and instead jumped from place to place, leaving him with no proper path to trace backwards from.

A tear rolled down her cheek as she leaned in and wrapped him in her arms. She didn't smell like flowers, in fact, she smelled like she hadn't showered in days. He didn't mind.

"I was so worried Leo; you have no idea," she wept, burying her head in his shoulder as the dam broke and all the emotion she had been trying so hard to mask burst forth at once, soaking into the fabric of his hospital gown.

It was several moments before she detached from him, but when she did, he was shocked at what he saw. For the first time, he was seeing Lucille Barett without makeup.

Her hair was a mess, her clothes were sweatpants and a ratty T-shirt. She was beautiful, perhaps more beautiful, but she might as well have been a different person entirely. How long had she been here with him? How many days?

"What... happened?" His eyes fluttered and closed. The light was too much to handle all at once. He still remembered that void, and after that perfect darkness, this faint light might as well have been the sun itself.

"You overdosed. You've been in and out of consciousness for three days. You flat-lined several times. They asked me Leo, they asked me what it was you might have taken, but I told them I didn't know. I told them a stranger gave them to you. It was those pills, right? Oh, I just know it was." She lifted her shaking hands to wipe the tears from her swollen red eyes.

"No," he muttered, shaking his head ever so slightly. "Someone... changed them. Not the same."

She blinked twice and then leaned in closer.

"What do you mean?"

"I took them, just like every night. But these were different. Rounder. Metallic. I knew it was wrong, but it was too late. Something bad happened... something... after me. They... they wanted to send a message."

Tears fell from her eyes, rolling down her cheeks, landing upon the blankets and splattering on the tile floor. He could tell from that look that she didn't believe him. Did he blame her? He was here, he almost died. She had been through it, watched it all from the right side of reality. Would he have believed her if the tables were turned?

"Leo, they want to discharge you to a psych ward. They think you're a danger to yourself." Her voice quivered as she spoke.

Leo smiled. "Maybe I am."

"No," Lucille shook her head and placed her hand against his cheek, "no, you just need help. I told them you would stay with me. The head doctor here is a friend of my father. I told them I would care for you. I don't want to hear a word about it Leo. This is final. I don't want to lose you again."

He stared into her eyes. She was the only person in the world, and for a moment the entire universe consisted of just them and that horrible beeping. Each time it beeped he struggled not to wince, but the sound, it was grating, horrible, terrible. He wanted to rip the machine apart piece by piece and then toss it from the tallest building.

"Mr. Harr," a voice echoed from out of view. Lucille turned and smiled, muttering the words "Doctor" followed by a name that Leo did not understand nor recognize.

A man entered the room, an older man, early sixties, his hair whiter than the sterile walls that surrounded them.

"Mr. Harr, I am Doctor Chapman. How are you feeling?"

Lucille might not have noticed it, but Leo did. That condemnation and judgment in the man's voice. It was in his eyes too, that look that said, "Here lies another drug addict. We should have let him die. Good riddance, I say."

Leo licked his lips. He wanted to spit, but his mouth was sand.

"Tired," was all he managed.

The doctor nodded and then turned his eyes towards the clipboard he held in his hands.

"So, the toxicology reports came back. You're clean, though I have no idea how. Besides high doses of nicotine, there isn't anything inside of you that shouldn't be there. At least not that we were looking for. Do you know what it was you took? Miss Barett here has informed us that there was some kind of mysterious pill involved. Perhaps it was something we don't currently test for."

Leo turned towards Lucille and shook his head. "I don't know. Lucille, did you go back to the apartment and get the bottle?"

She nodded, though the worry on her face was beyond apparent. "The Super let me in, but there was nothing there. We tore the place apart Leo. He was very worried for you. We both were. But there was nothing."

Why did that make sense? Why was that exactly what he expected her to say? Of course, it wouldn't be there. It wasn't for them. It wasn't for her. It was for him.

"I don't know what to tell you, doc."

The doctor sighed, his eyes darting between Lucille and Leo as he struggled to not only understand the dynamic of their relationship, but also why someone like her would involve herself with someone like him.

"Well Mr. Harr, we have several more tests to run. You did flat-line. Three times. So, we want to make sure there is no damage to your organs, and that there's no damage to your brain."

He paused, his eyes saying what his lips wouldn't. "Not like you have one of those to start with."

Leo smiled. They understood each other. The doctor continued, "but if all the tests come back negative, then you will be discharged into Miss Barett's care. She has informed us that you will stay with her. We recommended other accommodations, and would be happy to go over them with you if you are interested."

"Yea, I'll be staying with her." Leo smiled at the doctor. In his mind, he raised both hands and extended his middle fingers. In reality, he didn't move a muscle.

"Very good. Mr. Harr, you should rest. Miss Barett, I understand you are responsible for payment and billing?"

"Yes, doctor."

Leo's eyes darted between them. No, what was happening? She was paying for his medical bills? No, he needed to say something to stop this before it was too late. But it already was too late, and they were gone, out of the room, and he was alone once more. He sighed and stared towards the ceiling; his fists clenched tight by his side. He breathed deep, trying to calm himself, but all he felt inside was shame, regret, and rage.

CHAPTER 15

THE COLLAPSE

His legs felt like water, wiggling and writhing beneath him, shaking as he struggled to stay upright. Lucille held his shoulder, guiding him across the threshold into her home, or rather, his new home. Was this place truly a home? Or was this just a new prison? Better than the alternative, yet what freedoms would he really have here?

Leo stumbled and braced himself against the wall. Lucille gasped, but held strong, keeping him from colliding into an end table and an overly expensive vase. Everything was mush. His arms, his legs, his muscles, they all felt like pudding and he could do nothing about it. It had been two days since 'the incident'—as he referred to it in his mind— and yet he felt as weak as he had the moment he awoke.

She guided him into the room with the crimson carpet and lead him towards that vibrant red couch. Without a word, he collapsed into it and let it swallow him. His mind swirled, circling the drain as it hurdled towards sleep. He felt Lucille lift his legs and remove his shoes. He muttered something. She did not respond. His eyes fluttered open, filling with shades of red that threatened to overwhelm him. How long had it been since his vision was filled with such colors? He had always felt in colors, his emotions visible as shades of this or that, yet how long now since he had even seen a single a color at all? All this red was a thing of impossible beauty. So much color at once. He relished that moment; he let it consume him, let the red melt into him. He was the red. Just as it always should have been.

"Just rest Leo," Lucille's soft voice broke through the silence as she pressed her lips against his forehead. "Are you thirsty? Hungry? Is there anything you need?"

He shook his head, lifting his eyes and smiling up at her. That image of sexuality had transformed into something entirely different. The mask of Aphrodite had melted away, revealing Demeter beneath. She had always been there; it had always been her, disguised, hiding, luring him towards her. Aphrodite's face to get his attention, but Demeter's soul. Why was it then, that as he stared back at her he felt nothing but disgust?

He watched Lucille walk away, shutting the white doors behind her, leaving them only slightly cracked. He watched her leave, and he felt no affection, no desire, nothing but sadness and sorrow at losing his Aphrodite. What was causing this? Was it the shame he felt now that she had seen him for who he truly was? A fraud, an addict, a junkie? No, she knew who he was long before this. Was it disgust in knowing that he needed her, that he no longer had the benefit of wanting her, that she was his lifeline, his piggy bank, and he was doomed without her? Perhaps that was it. It wasn't fair. He knew it wasn't. Maybe it was just the exhaustion talking, maybe this red room, full of sexuality and passion, full of anger and rage, maybe this room could bring back the rest of the colors, and with those colors he could remake Aphrodite's mask and set it ever so carefully upon Demeter's motherly face.

Leo sighed and rolled over. He felt like a bus had hit him. His eyes scanned the walls, the floors, the furniture. Nothing had changed since the last time he had been in this room save the addition of a new painting on the wall. When had that been? Suddenly a memory sparked in the back of his mind. This had been where he answered the phone, where it had all truly begun. Why had he forgotten this place? His eyes fell upon a familiar painting that hung directly in front of the couch. That boat adrift in a turbulent black ocean. He smiled. That shade, that detailless figure in the boat morphed before him, slowly turning its head and smiling back at him with his own face, his own eyes, his own smile. He had almost forgotten about that painting.

His eyes fluttered and soon he was back in his own boat, in his own ocean, adrift on his own glass sea. The silence was perfect, the calm incredible. Here there was no pain, here there was no weakness, no sorrow, no Aphrodite or Demeter, no mental hospitals or strange pills. Here was only itself and itself was only now, and that thing, that place, that time, was perfect and it was everything.

Something moved beneath the waters. He could not see it, but he could see the ripples writhing across the glass-like surface. He leaned over the side of the boat, staring into a perfect reflection of his own form, but he saw nothing. No light penetrated that flawless surface. He paddled onward, moving towards the infinite horizon, moving not at all. There was no sense of motion, no sense of movement, no sense of time, or distance, or scale, but he moved nonetheless and as he moved further from those ripples, the calm returned.

Another series of ripples, somewhere far off, behind him. He felt them more than saw them. How was that possible? He turned his head in time to see them dissipate back into the calm, folding in upon themselves as they fell away, sinking into the waters. Was something here? Was something following him?

His heart rate increased, he was breathing faster now, sweating, gasping, his chest taught, his muscles aching as he paddled away from it. Fruitless and pointless. The ripples were ahead of him now. Small waves growing more severe. He watched their shape; he imagined the form of the thing that caused them, and it terrified him. He was terrified of everything, of the glassy waters above him, of the darkness below him, of the silence, of the calm, of the trembling darkness that seemed everywhere and nowhere. He was terrified of the light itself.

Leo lifted the paddles and placed them inside the boat. No water dripped from their wooden surface. Of course, it didn't. There was no water here. The water was nothing, and he was nothing and all of this was nothing and that nothing had substance and shape and that shape was his own that he had given it in his mind. He laughed aloud as he remembered where he was. This was his. His, not someone else's, not some other world, not a threshold to another dimension, his. That thought no longer comforted him and instead he remembered who he was, what lived and crawled and crept through his mind, and terror seized hold.

The waters rippled around him, churning, splashing, writhing. He saw it now, just below the surface, on the border of sight, right at the edge where the light barely touched. It was made of obsidian, darker than the blackness below it, a long sinewy form of a serpent that slid silently beneath the waters. It swallowed itself, again and again, a macabre scene of impossibility as it devoured its own tail, over, and over, and over again.

The waters rose, and the waves crashed against his boat. He was helpless and hopeless, trapped in the center of that swirling vortex of infinity. He had been all along, all his life, ever since he could remember. It had always trapped him, and there was nothing he could do, not now, not then, not ever. He was stuck, imprisoned just like the rest of them, just like all of them, just like everyone.

The waves beat against the boat and it groaned and creaked under the strain. Water seeped in through growing cracks, cold, warm, hot, tepid, burning and freezing his skin as it soaked him to the bone. He did not struggle this time, instead he merely watched that serpent devour itself forever, and ever, and ever, amen. He watched, and he waited, like the rest of them do, like all of them do, like they've always done, waiting for that serpent to tear him to tiny, imperceptible shreds.

A noise snapped Leo awake. His heart pounded, his hands shook, he was covered in sweat. The surrounding colors were darker now, still red, but red like the color of mostly dried blood. Dark, nearly black. Outside it was night. He had slept through the entire day. The only light streamed in from the hallway from some halogen bulb just outside the doors, just out of view. Something echoed in the distance, and his blood froze as the noise reverberated through the house.

Ring, Ring.

He wept, tears falling from his face, staining the red black. Not again, not anymore. Why him? Why not someone else, why could he not be normal? He felt it, that creeping feeling of insanity clawing away at the metal sheathing of his mind, searching for the wires that held him together. It was close to finding them, and when it did, he knew exactly what it would do. It would cut them all, sever the remaining ties between himself and reality, and he would lay here on this couch for eternity, drooling and staring at a piece of art he had once constructed. People would come see him, they would ask who he was, and others would point at the painting and say, "He made that you know. Back before he lost his mind." And they would all laugh, and they would pat him on the head like a dog, and he would drool, and moan, but he wouldn't be him any longer, he would be something else, dead inside, gone, lost forever.

Ring, Ring.

He could wait it out, he could pretend like he didn't hear it. He could lay there and wait, and maybe, just maybe it would stop. Had he tried that before? He struggled to remember.

Ring, Ring.

He laughed to himself as he muttered into the air a raunchy joke about a stripper and a priest. Where had he heard that one before? Oh, that's right. From a priest. Or had it been a stripper?

Ring, Ring.

It burned. The sound physically burned. It hurt him, inside and out, it penetrated everything. It didn't really ring; he understood that now; it vibrated inside of him. He was the phone; he was the ringing; it was all inside of him. What if he tore it out? What if he dug a hole in his chest cavity and removed the wires, and the receiver, and the telephone poles, and everything else that might connect that monstrosity to himself? What if he just put a bullet in his head and ended it? Would it still ring?

Ring, Ring.

That was his answer. He pictured it now. Himself laying a pile of gore and blood, his jaw hanging by a thread, a .45 in his limp hand, the stench of shit, piss, and burning flesh heavy on the air. And even as his brain fired off the final commands, the electric signals fading to nothing, his consciousness riding that split-second moment of eternity, he could still hear it.

Ring, Ring.

A joke, a macabre joke. What was his life anymore? It was not his own, that much was certain. Who was he? Leo Harr? No, Leo Harr was dead. They found him face down in a pile of his own vomit in an alleyway, surrounded by cats and feral dogs. No, they hadn't found him there. They had found him falling from the roof of a building, hurtling towards earth at terminal velocity as he slammed face first into the concrete, exploding into a thousand little Leos that all grew up to be artists and fought with each other, and yelled at each other, and made the same paintings and flooded the market with fakes and then died alone and forgotten.

Ring, Ring.

Leo jumped up from the couch and nearly collapsed. His legs were too weak, his body was still recovering. He didn't care. He knew where that phone was; he needed to get to it. He clenched his teeth and took a step.

White engulfed him. Painful, burning, horrible white. The sound, he had forgotten that sound. How could he have forgotten something so terrible? It lasted forever, for a thousand forevers, burning, peeling, scouring, unmaking him. He screamed and screamed, but there was nothing to scream with. There was nothing at all but the white.

He felt arms around him; he heard crying and sobbing, the eternity ended, and the white subsided, and he felt Lucille's soft hands caressing his cheek as she wept.

"It's three thirty, isn't it?"

She sobbed, and he wailed, and she groaned, and he wept with her. And no longer did Leo feel any affinity towards the long-lost Aphrodite. No, he realized now that it had been Demeter whom he loved all along. In that moment of a thousand tiny seconds, he rested his head against her chest, and he told her everything, from the very start, every detail, every minor thing, and they cried together until there was nothing left.

CHAPTER 16

THE HAUNTED

"You look like shit Leo." Joe's voice held no sarcasm, no humor, no hint of playfulness. He was deadly serious, and his eyes betrayed the concern that hid just behind his voice, shrouded by the slightest bit of apprehension.

"Thanks Joe. Means a lot." Leo wasn't in the mood for it. Not today. It had been what, a week since he had moved into Lucille's place? Today was the first day he had felt strong enough to move about. He had insisted–though it had taken much insisting– on walking to his apartment instead of being driven there. He was to pack up his things, clean the apartment out, scour it clean. The movers would arrive in a few hours to haul it all away. All of what had once been his life, his own sacred life, now part of her life instead. How had this happened? How had such a simple proposition of a one-night stand, made in a drunken haze, ended up like this? There were chains digging into him, her chains, or maybe someone else's. Either way, he didn't like the feeling.

"Hey, I'm not trying to be a dick, but I thought you looked bad last time I saw you, and just... yea. So, where you been? I was gettin' worried. Haven't seen you in about a week." Joe turned, reaching out to grab the pack of cigarettes, never taking his eyes off Leo. He didn't place the cigarettes down on the counter. Instead he held them, sliding them between his hands as he waited for Leo's reply.

Leo sighed and leaned up against the counter. "They say I overdosed. I cracked man. Lost it. Brain's fried, everything's a mess. They wanted to send me to a mental hospital, put me in a white padded room and all that. Medicate me until I was pissing myself and giggling about the fact that I'd been pissing myself. Friend of mine... girlfriend? I don't know what she is. Anyway, she offered to take care of me. Didn't really offer, I guess. Made the call while I was under. Don't know how they let it go through but you know, pretty women get whatever they want I guess."

"Please tell me you chose the broad over the padded cell." Joe nearly smiled, though the brevity was momentary and dissipated upon arrival.

"I did. Didn't have a choice, really. She decided, and so there it was. You won't see me for a while, or maybe ever. Who knows? All that shit I told you about, well its worse now, hasn't stopped. Damned dreams again, every fucking night. That phone, that light. She must love me, or love the attention, or something, because she's there, every single morning, 2:30 sharp, holding me while I scream and scream for an hour until that pain goes away." Leo closed his eyes. It was too much. It was all too much. He had been contemplating blowing his brains out every day since arriving at Lucille's. Today had been different though. Today he thought about being more creative, his mind fixated on how to turn a common suicide into a work of art. Oh, the scenes he could paint on traffic signs and brick walls with his blood.

"Doctors have any idea what's goin' on?" Joe wasn't convinced. His tone said as much. No, for some reason Leo knew that Joe believed him, or believed that he believed him. How much he really believed him was probably up for debate, but Joe was willing to entertain him, and that was enough.

"Clean as a horse. They say I overdosed right?" Leo chuckled to himself, pressing his fingers into his eyes before running his hands through his hair. He knew how crazy he looked but he didn't care. "But the blood tests all come back negative, nothing. That day it happened; someone swapped the pills. Something is after me. And it's trying to kill me." It was then that Leo realized he was shaking. He slipped his hands into his pockets and took a deep breath, scanning the store to make sure no one else had entered.

"You think it was whatever you were talkin' about last time?" Joe slid the pack of cigarettes across the counter and shook his head when Leo moved to grab his wallet. "On the house."

Leo muttered a thank you and snatched the pack off the counter, sliding it into his pocket like the cigarettes were gold. "There's something happening, man. They told me that something was after me, and I didn't listen and then all that stuff happened and I almost died, and I saw shit man, I saw dark shit. Not the devil. No. Worse than the devil. The devil, he has a face, right? This... this was the devil's father, and he has no face, and is nothing, and lives nowhere, and it's horrifying."

Joe relaxed back onto his stool and crossed his arms. This entire thing seemed to intrigue him. The worry and concern faded, replaced with genuine curiosity. "So, what you gonna do?"

"Well Joe, I'll tell you this much. Lucille won't let me drink, smoke, nothing. Water and vitamins, that's it. So, I'm supposed to go back up to my apartment and wait for the movers, and I'm gonna smoke this whole fucking pack before they get there. She can't stop me if she isn't there." His heart rate spiked he chuckled uncomfortably. Fear was creeping in. Fear as he watched the people passing the windows and watched the cars drive by. Every shape and form a possible enemy in disguise seeking to end him, to drag him back down to that bottomless abyss. He paused and turned his eyes toward Joe. What if Joe was one of them? What if these cigarettes were... what had that girl called them... a Double Meaning? Where did that memory come from? What little girl? He didn't know any little girls. The park. Yes, the park, and the bald man. They were the ones to blame. Or were they?

"I mean what are you gonna to do about bein' followed? You know how I told you about my brother? Killin' himself after he saw the aliens or whatever. Well, I didn't tell you the whole story. See, he said he was bein' followed too, and the story is that he did it to himself. Ended it, just couldn't handle the fuckin' stress or whatever. They say he snapped, but I know my brother. He didn't kill himself man. Fucker didn't have it in him, no matter how crazy he might have been at the end. Besides, who ever heard of shooting yourself dead center in the back of the head?"

Leo stared at Joe as the words curled and licked against his ears, slipping down into his brain, permeating his psyche and consciousness, morphing his entire sense of what was real and what was fake. So Joe had never thought his brother was crazy at all. Joe had believed him. Joe believed Leo too. Maybe he wasn't going insane, maybe there really was something else going on after all.

"I..." Leo started, but the words fell away. What was he going to do? Did he have a plan? "I don't know. I can't trust anyone man. Well you and Lucille, but anyone else out there, they could be one of them. I've seen it, man. I've spoken to them as an old man and a little girl. They change dude, they change bodies, or shapes, or 'Reality Boxes' they call them. It's insanity is what it is, it's fucking insanity, and I'm insane. I can't live like this man." Leo was begging, pleading for help, but he knew Joe couldn't help him. Joe was doing all he could, and that would have to do.

"You can live like this because you fuckin' have to." Joe's words rang through the store, echoing against the beer fridges and soda bottles, breaking apart into a thousand voice chorus that sang back at him. "Look man," Joe leaned forward, "I watched my brother go through this. And I never told nobody this, but I believe he did see something. Everyone always thinks I'm stupid. But I ain't stupid. I watch things, see shit nobody else sees. And if you're gonna to tell me that we, that this, is all there is. Then you're the one who's fuckin' stupid. Now, you got any idea how to stop this?"

Leo felt like he was in an '80s action movie. Like he and Joe were about to suit up and hunt vampires and save the world, get the girl, and make everything right again. Except that's not how it would go, was it? He already had the girl, and Joe wasn't going to leave his store, and there were no vampires. Just shades of madness hiding in shadows behind the corners of his mind, folding into his gray matter as they dug and delved deeper and deeper, burrowing down, down, until there was nothing left to dig at. Tearing and shredding until his brain was mush and he was face down in a gutter blubbering about 'colors' and 'triangles' and 'the ringing phone'.

"I have to close the red door." Leo said it so matter-of-factly that he nearly startled himself.

Joe only nodded. "Then go close the fuckin' door and get on with your life." With that, he slapped his hands down on the counter and jumped off the stool. "I got sandwiches to make. That damn vegan meat came in earlier. Fun shit. You can see how excited I am, see? Yea, I'm fuckin' thrilled. Look, you got this man. And I am goin' to see you again. And when I do, and it's all over, we're goin' out for some drinks, my treat."

Just like that, Joe was on to something else. The metaphysical nature of the conversation took no toll on him, the mind-bending concepts simply rolled off him as if they had been talking about sports or the weather. To Joe, this was just another conversation. To anyone else, this would have seemed like pure and unadulterated madness. Leo smiled and muttered a final goodbye to his friend. Yes, Joe was his friend, a fact he never realized until that very moment. Perhaps, if not for all of this, he never would have realized it, but he realized it now, and that was what mattered.

The bell dinged and Leo exited the convenience store, peeling the plastic off the cigarettes as he pulled one to his lips and lit it. That taste was exactly what he needed.

He whistled while he walked towards his apartment. The light was different, it was always different now, ever since 'the incident', but there was a vibrant glow on the fringes he hadn't seen in over a week. He felt alive, he felt free. The claws and chains that wrapped around him were gone for the moment, and Leo Harr was a free man and the city was his.

"Leo Harr!" The voice echoed from the other side of the road. Leo turned his head towards the sound. Panic gripped his chest. He tossed the cigarette to the ground. Why did he do that? Was he that afraid that Lucille might see him smoking? He was a grown man. He scanned for the source of the voice, but he saw no one.

His breathing quickened; his chest tightened. He lowered his head and pressed forward, ducking around the corner, his head on a swivel, constantly checking behind him.

"Leo Harr, we must speak!" He saw the source of that voice and nearly vomited where he stood. That brown hat, that bald head, that featureless fucking face. No, no, no. It needed to leave him alone, they all needed to leave him alone.

He sped up, dipping into an alleyway, cutting through a shortcut before doubling back and then ducking into another alleyway. How could he trust any of them? How did he know this featureless man was the same featureless man as before? The triangle had given him no code, nothing to prove its identity. It couldn't, not anymore, not since the medicine went missing.

What if he stopped running? What if he asked the man for more medicine? But how could he know it was the right medicine? How could he know anything without the code? The codes were all he had, the only things that he knew for a fact were true. Everything else could be those obsidian faces of perfect nothingness trying to claw at him in the nether. He would never know, not without a code, not without the phone. But he couldn't answer the phone anymore. He was lost.

"Leo Harr! Please, we must speak with you!" The voice was closer now. How? The man was walking slower than Leo but gaining ground at an incredible pace. Leo wound through another alley, his heart exploding in his chest. He would die like this, right here, of a cardiac arrest, and when they found him there would be no bald man or pile of strange pills, there would be nothing. Just a dead man. And they would wonder how he died, and no one would ever know, and they would ask friends and family about him and everyone would say, "oh that guy, yea, he really lost it there before the end."

Leo rounded the last turn and slid his keys from his pocket. He fumbled with them, grasping for the right one as the footsteps closed in behind him. Time slowed to a crawl as he slid the key in first try. The lock clicked open. He pushed through the door and slammed it shut behind him. He was covered in sweat, shaking, quivering, tears rolling down his face as he watched that featureless man round the bend and stand before the glass door, his entire form filling the window.

"Leo Harr!" the man yelled, though he made no motion to break in or smash the glass. Leo searched those eyes, those eyes that were just too plain, just too normal to be human. Was this They? Or was this some other They from some other place? He couldn't risk it.

"Leave!" Leo yelled through the glass. "I don't know you! Leave me alone!"

"Leo Harr!" The man called in response. "You are in great danger! They know where are you are! They are coming for you! Leo Harr! Communication has been broken; we must repair the line!"

With that, the man held up a translucent orange bottle of oblong pills. They looked identical to the ones from before, but how could he know for certain? Leo's eyes darted from the pill bottle to the man's face and back again. He couldn't trust any of them, not anymore. No, this was bigger than it had been, more significant. Something hunted him, and those hunters could come in any form, and those pills could take him anywhere.

Leo shook his head, slowly at first, then frantically as tears fell from his eyes. "I can't! I can't trust any of you!" He yelled, collapsing into a heap as he crawled away from the door in terror.

The shapes, the black shapes. He could see them on his periphery, clawing their way in, digging towards that perfect inverted triangle. They would smash it to smithereens. He could stop this, but how did he know who was who and what was what? He was powerless, he could do nothing, and so he simply curled up, eyes staring unblinking at the featureless figure outside the door.

"Leo Harr! Please!" The man cried. Was there panic in his voice? His eyes darted to the side. Terror, or some kind of emotion–negative and fearful–filled his eyes. He cast one final glace at Leo and fled without a trace, taking that translucent bottle of pills with him.

It was in that moment, as Leo held himself and shook, rocking back and forth on the filthy tile floor beneath the row of mailboxes, that he realized he had been wrong. That the man had been They, the real They, and those pills, that offering, that had been his last chance, and he had let it go, and it was gone, and now Leo Harr was truly all alone, and there was nothing to stop those obsidian figures. They would break through, and they would smash that triangle, and all that was good and beautiful would collapse to nothing, and everything would die, and now there was nothing he could do to stop it.

CHAPTER 17

THE SUPER

"Leo?" A warm voice, a man's voice, a familiar voice, broke through the noise and the fear. It was far away and concerned. Whose voice was it, though? Leo trembled, huddling against the cold tile and peeling wallpaper. He dared not open his eyes, he dared not let the pictures in. What might they show him?

He couldn't trust his own eyes anymore; he knew that now. Maybe he couldn't trust his mind either. They were playing tricks on him, conjuring images, inventing people, inventing paranoias and fears. There was nothing to be afraid of, it was all in his head. He understood that now. He had figured it all out as he huddled in that corner. Was there anything at all? Was he even alive? No, he was dead and condemned to hell. This was his punishment. When had he died? Perhaps it had been long ago, back at that party, back when Tori left him. Yes, that was it. When Tori left him. It had all been downhill from there.

"Leo? Are you okay?" The voice was closer now, approaching on reverberating footsteps that echoed down the halls. In the darkness behind his eyelids Leo saw those sounds; he saw them bouncing endlessly until entropy destroyed them, unraveling them, disintegrated them, utterly and completely crushing them within its unrelenting grasp.

A hand touched his shoulder, a heavy hand, a rough hand. Leo shuddered and cowered away. Was this the end? Had they come for him again? Would they let him leave now that they found him? The hand rested there, squeezing lightly. No, this wasn't the end, this was not the enemy.

Leo opened his eyes, half-expecting to see that strange featureless man in his large brown hat standing over him. His vision focused; the blurry male form taking shape like smoke coalescing into physical form. Leo felt the tension release from his muscles as he beheld Mr. Russo, the Super. He hovered over Leo; knees bent into a crouch. He wore an old mechanic's shirt, the name Mario embroidered in a patch above his left breast pocket. If there was anyone who fit the stereotype of middle-aged Italian landlord, it was Mr. Russo. From his hair, to his facial features, to his mustache, you could have picked the man up and dropped him into any Italian neighborhood in

New York and someone would instantly greet him as their uncle.

"Leo? Hey kid, you okay?" Mr. Russo's voice was calm, but behind his eyes Leo could see the beginning signs of panic as those dark filaments of fear reached inward, beginning to grab hold.

Leo blinked and shifted, unfurling himself as he rose into a seated position against the wall. The paranoia fled, disappearing as quickly as it had come. For a moment he couldn't even remember why he had been paranoid. Where was he? The row of mailboxes behind the Super were familiar. He recognized his own. That's right, he had fled in here from that man, that strange featureless man. But why? Why had he run from him? He rubbed his eyes and shook his head, shame and embarrassment washing over him. He felt like a fool.

"Sorry Mr. Russo. Yea, I'm ok. I just..." Did he dare lie? He recalled Lucille's story of how she and the Super went into his apartment together to look for the pills. Mr. Russo knew what had happened, he knew Leo was unhinged. No, there was no point to lying. "I had a bit of a mental break. But I'm okay. I get paranoid from time to time. I'm sorry for doing it here like this."

How much more insane did he sound trying to explain it so matter-of-factly? People must think he was an absolute lunatic. They wouldn't be wrong though.

"It's ok, Leo, I'm just worried about you is all. You need anything? Water, something to eat?" The Super rose to his feet, but his eyes never left Leo. He studied him like a child studying a gorilla at the zoo. Leo was an anomaly, a harmless anomaly, one everyone wanted to get a good hard look at. Maybe they would be the one to understand what made him tick.

"Water would be great," Leo nodded, taking a deep breath as he tried to relax his pounding heart. He had struggled with panic attacks as a child, but this was different. This was like reality crumbling around him, like the earth beneath his feet had swallowed him and there was nothing he could do but fall in that endless nothing until time ceased to exist. It was horrible. No doubt the doctors would want to prescribe him some kind of anti-psychotic to make these episodes stop. That's all they ever wanted to do, prescribe some other pill, and if that didn't work, here's another one, or maybe try this, or how about all three at once. You're a zombie? Oh well, the problem's gone, so now it's all high fives and hero talk. We did it, we saved the world.

"Yea, I'll go grab you a bottle." Mr. Russo moved down the hall, casting a quick glance backwards before disappearing through the door marked 'Maintenance'.

Leo didn't try to stand. He just sat there. How many people had walked by and seen him there? How long had he been laying there? Had the movers already come? He glanced towards the glass door. The light didn't seem any different from when he entered. Perhaps an entire day had passed, or maybe only a few minutes. He had no way of knowing.

"Yea, Lucille?"

The voice was Mr. Russo's echoing from the main-tenance room. The Super was trying to be quiet, but the sheer silence of the building made that impossible. These tile floors carried sound, and from Leo's position in the corner he could hear everything clear as day.

"Hey, it's Mario Russo, Leo's Super? Yea, hey."

There was a pause.

"No, no, he's fine… I think. I found him huddled in the corner by the mailboxes. He was shaking."

Another pause.

Anger welled up inside of Leo. Why was it Lucille's business what he was doing? And why did the Super feel it was his place to contact her? No, it was good Mr. Russo cared that much, and it was good Lucille knew about it. He needed help; Leo knew it, but he hated to admit it. Some-thing was wrong, and he was broken. It would take every-one's help to put him back together again.

"I see."

"No, I don't think he fell."

"No, he didn't say anything about that."

"Oh, I see, so this…"

"Okay. I understand, I'll be easy with him."

What did that mean? Was she telling the Super that Leo was crazy? Well, he was crazy, but that wasn't anyone's business but his own. Even if he was crazy, she still shouldn't be telling people. And either way, he didn't want Lucille to think of him as crazy, that just made him feel crazier. Or was he crazy because he was analyzing one half of a conversation, writing in Lucille's parts from pure imagination? Maybe that's what really made him crazy.

"Yea, I just wanted to let you know, it was just strange, and I remembered what you told me."

"When will that be?"

"Sounds good, I'll let them up. Will you be with them?"

"Not a problem, I'll keep an eye on him."

"No worries, Lucille. Hey, you have a good day okay?"

"Yea, you too."

The one-sided conversation ended, and the door opened, revealing the form of Mr. Russo, his hand clutching an ice-cold bottle of water that dripped with condensation. Leo turned his face away. He was ashamed to make eye contact with the man.

"Hey here you go Leo." Mr. Russo handed the bottle over, breaking the bottle-top seal as he did so. "You sure you're good?"

Leo nodded, still averting his gaze as he took the bottle and downed it in one gulp. The icy water shocked his system, and he nearly burst out in a coughing fit. He hadn't realized how thirsty he was.

"Hey thanks for this Mr. Russo." Leo half smiled, his eyes still turned towards the floor, or the mailboxes, or the door, never focusing on the Super's face.

"No worries, kid." With that one word, Leo suddenly felt as if his father was the one checking in on him. Why did that make him feel even worse?

"Yea, I'm fine, I really am." Leo rose to his feet, eyes darting every which way to avoid looking at the Super. "Hey, I appreciate it. I really do. I have to go pack up my things. The movers will be here soon."

"Yea I'll let them in when they get here. I have to say Leo, I'm sorry to see you go. You may never have paid on time, but you were one of the best tenants I've had in my twenty years of owning this place."

This time Leo did look at him. The man was serious. His face and eyes glowed with a pride that Leo didn't understand. Leo hadn't paid his rent on time a single month in the three years he had lived there, and before Lucille had bought that painting he was one-month shy of eviction. How was it possible that someone would consider him to be a good tenant?

"Hey, I'm sorry about always being late. I should have paid, or left sooner. It wasn't fair, or right."

Mr. Russo smiled and slapped Leo on the shoulder. "Kid, that's what makes you a good tenant and a good person. You care. Most of my tenants, they're all late, but not one of them apologizes. They act entitled. You always apologized, always tried. It wasn't a lot, it didn't pay the bills, but it meant more than you think. Take care of yourself out there, kid."

With that, Mr. Russo turned and disappeared back into the maintenance room. Leo stood alone in the hall; an empty water bottle clutched in his hand. If the world could make sense for even a single moment, it would be a miracle. Leo shook his head and fumbled in his pocket for his keys as he began the ascent towards his apartment.

Darkness struggled to break in on the fringes of his periphery, but he held it back. That paranoia, he could feel it, still there, clawing at him, but he wouldn't let it win again. Not like it had. No, he would keep fighting. He had to.

Leo stopped at the top of the stairs and turned, looking back towards the front door. He half-hoped to see that strange man still standing outside the door, waving the translucent bottle of pills. But he wasn't there, and Leo had this sinking feeling that he wasn't going to return. That darkness on his periphery closed ever so slightly as the realization set in that there were, in fact, people after him, people he couldn't see, people he didn't know, people that weren't people, and he was alone to fight them.

Leo stopped at his apartment door and unlocked it, allowing it to swing open freely as the room beyond revealed itself. This would be the last time he looked upon this view, the last time he entered this apartment, the last time he stepped foot inside of a place that was his, at least for a very long time.

He stepped through the threshold and his eyes darted towards the counter where the bottle of pills had once stood. Why had he half expected to find them right where he left them?

He lifted the mattress, but the bottle wasn't there. He got on his hands and knees and searched under the bed and the furniture, peeling away the couch cushions, looking for the bottle inside of vases and old boxes. He tore the place apart in search of that bottle of pills. But just as Lucille had said, it was gone.

He closed his eyes and for a brief moment he could see that radiant triangle in his mind's eye. Would he ever see it again? The memory was fading, even now it wasn't as vibrant as it had been. The colors, they were his colors now, reds, pinks, blues, purples. He couldn't remember what the other colors had felt like.

Leo sighed and collapsed upon the couch as he slid a cigarette into his mouth and lit it. He still had to finish the entire pack before the movers arrived. Leaning his head back, Leo watched the smoke curl and dance in the air. He didn't care that he wasn't packing or that the movers would be there soon, or that Lucille might catch him smoking. It felt nice not to care. Like a warm shower on a chilly day, it was just what he needed.

CHAPTER 18

THE DISCOVERY

The couch was the last thing to go, carried away on the backs of several young men—no doubt college students trying to earn extra money—who struggled to maneuver it through the too-small doorway. They succeeded eventually, taking the final piece of Leo's freedom with them. The room was bare, completely devoid of ornamentation or furniture, save for a single piece of art that Leo had left behind for the next tenant. An inverted pyramid, black and deep purple, surrounded by a vibrant fiery rainbow.

Lucille hadn't liked the idea, in fact she referred to the painting as "disturbing" and made sure to always keep her back to it, or keep it just out of sight since entering the apartment. It made Leo smile. Maybe he needed to bring it with him to her house, to keep her away when he wanted some of his freedom back.

"You ready, dear?" Her once-angelic voice screeched through the air like a harpy, clawing against his ears like nails on a chalkboard. Since when had he grown to hate her so much? Hadn't it only been two weeks since the exhibition? How had so much changed so fast?

She didn't even talk to him the same anymore. That mask of sexuality had peeled away, revealing nothing beneath. She was lonely, normal, plain. The sexuality was a lure and once she caught her prey, she no longer needed it. Leo chuckled to himself. All this, all the living together, the money, the talking to each other like a married couple, and they hadn't even had sex yet.

"I'm going to walk," he muttered; his eyes still focused on the painting that hung so stark against the plain gray wall.

"Leo dear, that's not a good idea. Come, lets drive together." There it was. The sexuality was back. A lure, a hook to get what she wanted and drag him in. No, it wouldn't work, not this time.

"I'm going to walk," Leo repeated, eyes never moving from the painting. His muscles and chest tightened; his body readied itself for a fight.

"If you insist, dear."

The fight never came. He relaxed and took a deep breath. How much of his hatred for Lucille was warranted? Surely not much, if any. She had done nothing but try to help him, done nothing but be there for him in his darkest times, and yet he responded by hating her. Perhaps it wasn't her he hated, perhaps it was himself.

"I just need some fresh air to clear my mind. It's not too far." Maybe he resented her because they hadn't had sex yet, because she had promised it so many times in the way she spoke and carried herself, and yet it never happened. Maybe he was just frustrated.

Lucille stepped forward, clutching her purse and leaning her head against his shoulder. She smelled like flowers, a smell that carried him away from this place, far away, to a field in the middle of nowhere. In that place where there was only her and him, and they were naked, and the breeze was cool.

"What made you paint that?" There was something strange in her tone, something accusatory and condescending hiding behind the playful and innocent. Leo could almost see the words exit her mouth, sticky black things that oozed from her lips.

"It's the closest I could get to the actual thing."

She knew about it all. He had told her everything, from the start of it to the present. He hadn't told her about the man following him earlier in the day, though. That would remain his and his alone. He had seen how she reacted to the rest of the story, and he wasn't certain telling her more would be productive.

Her face had remained calm through the entire tale, calm and placid, her eyes focused on his as she took in every word, but there had been something beneath, something dark, something resentful and angry, something bitter just beneath the surface that he couldn't get more than a glimpse of. It was that same darkness that peaked out just now when she asked about the painting, the same hatred, the same disgust. Why was it there, and what was it? He had no answers, and that frustrated him.

"It's scary. It will probably scare the next people who move in here." Those were the words she said, but the words he heard were "It's disgusting. It doesn't belong, it needs to be destroyed." Was it something in her tone, or was he projecting?

"It's beautiful," he replied, his voice a whisper.

Lucille lifted her head and turned towards him. He could see the accusatory glare even out of the corner of his eye. "You've never spoken about me that way," it said, but her lips remained still and she said nothing. Maybe that's what it was. Maybe she was resentful that something else could compare, no, eclipse her own beauty. It would make sense. Lucille Barett was a conceited woman.

"I must be going Leo dear, and you need to as well. I still don't think it's a good idea for you to walk the streets alone, especially not after what happened earlier."

Leo smiled and turned towards her. For a moment he saw a shadow where her face was, a dark void that disappeared with a blink.

"I know the Super called you. Did you tell him I'm crazy?" His voice was poison, spraying into her face and eating her flesh away until there was nothing but bone.

She reeled back, pain flashing in her eyes as the words slapped against her cheek. "Leo, no. I would never." The sincerity was sickening, not because it was feigned, but because it was genuine. "I just told him you've been having episodes like that, and the doctors don't know what's going on. He was worried about you, Leo. I was worried about you."

Oh, how a mere change in tone can move the heart. All she needed to do was linger on one syllable too long, roll a letter, hang a pause on the air, all done just the right way and suddenly Leo's hormones were raging like he was a teenage boy. He sunk into those eyes, falling into them, consumed by them. All he wanted was her. It's all he ever wanted. She was his everything. How could there be anything but her? This perfect goddess loved him, and here he was condemning her, judging her, hating her. How stupid could he truly be?

"I'm sorry, Lucille." He hung his head and averted his eyes. No, he couldn't look at her, not after what he had done. He had to seek penance, had to find forgiveness and make it up to her somehow. She was a goddess, and he was a worm, he had no right to be standing in her presence much less speaking to her. How dare he look upon such beauty and perfection, how dare he lust after her, how dare he desire her.

"Oh Leo," Lucille leaned down, placing her purse on the floor as she wrapped her arms around his neck and drew him close. "I care about you so much. I know this is so hard on you. You will get through it. I'll be here with you through everything."

Leo lifted his arms and drew her in. He closed his eyes as he breathed in her scent; he rubbed his face against her hair and his hands against her back. This was the only place he ever wanted to be. This was heaven.

His eyes fluttered open as he kissed her hair, then buried his face in her shoulder. Life was exhausting, it all was, everything. He felt like a massive weight was pressing down on him, his back crumbling beneath the pressure. How long could he hold out until he snapped under the strain of his own fragile psyche?

His eyes darted across the room, studying the corners and curves, remembering memories that would now be forever isolated to his crumbling mind. How long until he completely forgot about this place? A month, a year, a decade? Eventually the memory of this apartment would be the memory of somewhere else, superimposed onto the vague image of its shape, and he wouldn't know the difference.

Something shimmered in the air, something that caught his attention. Leo's gaze fell upon Lucille's purse, a white and black thing, slight and small, probably worth more than a new car. An orange glimmer, barely visible, shone from deeper inside the purse, illuminated by the sunlight that streamed in unevenly through the windows. He stared at the purse, eyes focusing on that orange glimmer, and his heart raced. He knew that shine; he knew that color. As his eyes focused, and the darkness inside her bag became less obtrusive, the image of the thing came into view. It was the bottle of pills, his bottle of pills, that translucent orange bottle he had been searching for, the one he had been told was lost. He strained his eyes to see the shape of those pills, to see if they were oblong or rounded, but they were too far away and too small.

The world around him exploded into a thousand tiny fragments. She said she couldn't find them, yet here they were stuffed into her purse in such a way that he wouldn't see them. But he had. She was hiding them from him; she was lying to him. He pulled away, his eyes falling upon her face briefly before he averted his gaze.

Suddenly she was Medusa, her hair a mess of writhing serpents that slithered atop each other, wrapping themselves around her head and flicking their tongues into the air. He dared not look at her, not for long. She had broken his trust; she had lied; she had betrayed him. Aphrodite's mask shattered in that brief glance, as did Demeter's beneath, revealing nothing but a faceless, featureless obsidian shape. He blinked, and it was gone. Was he projecting again? No, not this time.

Leo opened his mouth to speak, but snapped it closed. Better not say anything. He needed to keep his own secrets now that he knew she was keeping hers. Lucille didn't seem to notice his change in demeanor. She simply retrieved her bag and smiled at him.

"I'll see you at home, dear, don't take too long." With those words she turned and exited the apartment, heels clicking against hardwood as her curves undulated beneath her tight white dress. Leo hardly noticed. The view should have enticed him, should have driven him mad with lust and desire, instead it merely fueled the hatred raging inside of him.

He watched her leave, standing silent and still until the clicking of her heels disappeared behind the closed door. She was gone, but was she truly gone? No, he would have to go back to where she was, and she would be there, she was always there. He couldn't trust her, not anymore. Or could he? Perhaps she had lied to keep him safe. Maybe she thought she had been doing the right thing, maybe she was trying to protect him? No, she had lied. She had lied to the doctors, and she had lied to him. That darkness just beyond the surface was real, he knew it now. There was something underneath the beautiful sexuality of Lucille Barett that was malicious, dark, and destructive. What was it? He had to know; especially now, but how would he ever peel away that mask? She was good, too good perhaps, cunning and quick. She would never let him strip it away.

Leo reached into his coat pocket and snatched the pack of cigarettes. The box was crushed, but the three cigarettes inside were preserved. He hadn't finished the pack before the movers came, but he had plenty of time to finish it on his walk back. Hell, who cared if she found out. Maybe if she realized he had secrets; he could confront her about her own.

He flicked the lighter twice and the flame ignited. Walking towards the open door, he turned and cast one final glance into the room, his eyes darted straight towards the painting. It was all that mattered; it was the only thing he could trust. As he closed and locked the door to his apartment for a final time, all he could think about was the red door, that blood red door hanging in the void of perfect nothingness. Joe's words rang out in his mind with perfect clarity, as if he was replaying a recording.

"Close the fuckin' door, and get on with your life."

He needed to find it again. He needed to end all of it, and then maybe, once it was over, he would be able to get his life back. Maybe he could then free himself of Lucille's chains and run wild once more.

CHAPTER 19

THE MOTIVATION

Cigarette hanging halfway out of his mouth, ash falling like embers as the paper and tobacco slowly burned away, Leo descended the staircase for the final time. Three years of memories. Three years of this staircase being part of his home. No longer.

The keys dug into his palm, his keys, but not his keys anymore. Two plain and unadorned silver keys that he had never paid attention to suddenly mattered more than anything. Giving up these keys meant sealing the lock on his own cage, locking himself in with Lucille. For how long? Forever? The image of that pill bottle ever so slightly visible in her purse haunted him, flashing before his vision on repeat. He was locking himself up with a liar. What good could come of this?

Leo took that irreversible step down onto the tile landing, his eyes darting towards the glass door, still half-expecting to see the strange man waiting for him. No one was there. Of course, they weren't. He had sent the man away. Why had he done something so foolish? It was a question he could apply to most of his life, and a question whose answer lay within itself. Because he was a fool.

Shoes clicking against the tile, Leo stepped towards the maintenance room. He knocked lightly before turning the knob and swinging open the door. Mr. Russo sat before a small, old-fashioned black-and-white TV watching reruns of '50s television shows from the comfort of his worn out, and thoroughly stained, blue office chair. The thing consisted more of duct tape than its original faux leather, but it wasn't broken so there was no need to replace it. At least that's what Mr. Russo always said when Leo asked about it.

"Hey Mr. Russo. Here are the keys." Leo extended his hand, the keys jingling as they tapped together.

The Super turned, his eyes widening as they instantly focused on the still-burning cigarette hanging from Leo's mouth. "Uh, kid, there's no smoking allowed in here." His voice wavered with uncertainty, as if part of him didn't care, and the other part was furious.

Leo removed the cigarette and scanned the room for somewhere to put it out. Finding nowhere, he placed it back in his mouth and shrugged. "Sorry Mr. Russo, I forgot. Here, I'll leave these with you and I'll be on my way."

The Super rose from the chair, extending his hand to receive the keys. For a moment Leo held on, unwilling to give up that ultimate symbol of his freedom. His hand shook, grasping the keys tighter before finally dropping them into the Super's palm. The bandage ripped off. The moment of pain was over.

"Well, I wish I had some profound words for you, kid. Just be careful out there. And watch out for your girl, she's a firecracker, that one. She'll eat you up and spit you out before you know what happened." Mr. Russo's eyes kept darting towards the cigarette. He endured the smoke, but it was obvious he wasn't pleased.

Leo smiled and nodded at the advice, doing his best to ignore the dirty looks. "How does that song go? She's a man-eater?" Leo laughed, ash flying into the air like snow. "Well, it is what it is. Thanks for everything, Mr. Russo."

The Super half-smiled. Leo wasn't certain if it was because of the cigarette, the incident earlier, or Lucille. Combined, all three things painted a wonderful picture of who Leo Harr was when no one was looking. What a way to sign off, to say goodbye, to end a relationship.

Leo turned away from the Super and exited the maintenance room, his eyes focused on the light beyond the glass door. That had been strange, Mr. Russo's mention of Lucille. He thought Mr. Russo held her in esteem, especially after calling her about Leo's condition earlier, but now he wasn't so certain. Maybe the man saw what Leo was just beginning to. That darkness behind the pretty face, the manipulative way she spoke, the lies in the way she moved.

Mr. Russo had been around long enough, no doubt he had seen his fair share of women like Lucille. Maybe the warning was from some personal memory of his, something he learned from his own Lucille decades before. That's the thing about women like her, they think they're unique, and they act special. Everyone treats them like they are because their beauty is overwhelming, but when the dust settles and the party's over, you can find a dozen men sharing stories about their own Lucille, each one drowning their sorrow in some kind of intoxicant, trying to forget–as much as remember–the way she moved.

The image of the orange pill bottle peaking from her purse flashed in his mind once more. Even having seen that, Leo knew he couldn't judge her. No, her face was too perfect, her curves too incredible, her flowing movements too graceful. He would always give her the benefit of the doubt. That's just the way it was, that's just the effect that she had on him. He wanted to hate her, and in a way, he did hate her, but she could make him love her, so what did it matter? Hate, love, it wasn't up to him. He was a puppet, and that was that.

A stiff wind snagged his coat, trying to peel it off his shoulders as he passed through the doorway. Why was winter still here? Why would spring not show itself? Leo tossed the burnt-out cigarette into the street as he lit another. What month was it anyway? What day of the week?

He had no sense of when, and as he started down the side-walk, he quickly lost the sense of where.

"Mr. Harr?" A woman's voice, young, soft, pretty, floated up from behind him. His muscles tensed. Who was this? Was this one of them? Or maybe this was They, back in another form?

Exhaling a cloud of blue-gray smoke, Leo turned. Before him, about thirty feet away, dressed in skin-tight leggings and a long overcoat, a vaguely familiar woman approached him, her mouth wide in a smile. She was pretty, not beautiful like Lucille, but pretty. Her blonde ponytail bobbed as she walked, floating up and around her face as the wind caught hold of it.

Where had he seen this woman before and how did she know him? He felt his pores open as the sweat flowed, running down his neck and his back, soaking into fabric under his armpits and around his waistline.

"I'm glad I caught you!" She exclaimed, vibrant green eyes sparkling in the sun. "I've tried several times, but you never seem to be home. I tried calling too, I hope you don't mind, but your phone kept going to voice-mail."

Call him? The mention of a call reminded him of the phone. Was this They? No, no, the features were too human, too memorable. Besides, he recognized her from somewhere, he just couldn't pinpoint where. Staring for a moment, the fear took hold. Merely the mention of a tele-phone had done so much to unnerve him. She wasn't threatening, she was simply standing still, kindly waiting for him to reply with some statement of familiar greeting.

He took a half-step backwards, still uncertain why this almost-familiar stranger was approaching him here on the sidewalk. She wasn't a stranger; he knew he had seen her before; he recognized the voice, but for the life of him he couldn't remember who she was, no matter how long he stared at her.

"I'm sorry, who are you?" He muttered between puffs of the cigarette, blowing the smoke towards her, though the wind carried it back into his own face.

She took a step forward, then paused, cocking her head to the side as she looked him up and down. It seemed his question had thrown her off; she seemed no longer certain if he was who she thought he was.

"Connie, from Dr. Ipsom's office." Her voice wavered a bit as a hint of fear lit up behind her eyes. She was questioning herself, asking herself if she had made some terrible mistake. Maybe she had. Leo wasn't the same person she had seen two weeks ago. No, he was different now. What did she want with him, anyway?

"Oh yea, sorry. The light's weird out here. How are you?" The words were an attempt to play it off, but his tone did nothing to achieve that effect. Level and devoid of emotion, he sounded like a robot, startling even himself with the amount of apathy that weighed those simple words down, pressing them towards the concrete.

"Uh, well," her smile faltered, but then returned. She was studying him, questioning herself, wondering if she should leave. Yes, flee, flee from here if you know what's good for you. Flee far, far away and forget the name

Leo Harr, forget his face, forget he existed. "I wanted to take you up on your offer."

What offer? What was she talking about? He took another drag off the cigarette. Was she losing her mind too?

"Offer?" He scratched his cheek as a sudden shadow sprinted across the corner of his vision. His eyes flicked towards the sky. Just a bird flying on the wind. Just a bird. The black shadow had startled him. Everything startled him these days. The darkness was right there, just on the edge of his vision. He couldn't lose his concentration else it would collapse in on him. If only he had that pill bottle, hiding, taunting him from the inside of Lucille's purse. A spark of rage ignited. He hated Lucille. Connie's face morphed before him, transforming into Lucille's. Suddenly, looking upon that perfect face, he didn't hate her anymore. He craved her, desired her, needed her. God, he loved Lucille so much.

"Yes, to paint me. You… You wanted to paint me, and I couldn't before because you were a patient, but you aren't anymore, I guess… I mean I hadn't seen you and Dr. Ipsom told me to remove you from the system, so I thought… well… that I'd take you up on your offer. I've always wanted to model."

She was so innocent, so naïve. He could hear it in her voice. She had trusted him and taken the offer at face value. No, the painting was just the foreplay. He had intended to sleep with her, to use his art, to use the guise of painting to get her naked and take her to bed. But she hadn't realized that, had she? No, this was innocence, pure innocence and trust. Better for her to leave, to forget she had ever met such a vile monster such as himself. He was no better than Lucille, was he? She used her beauty, but he used his talents. All to achieve the same means. That's why he and Lucille had ended up together, because they deserved each other.

"I, um... I actually can't. I have to stop painting for a while. There's this... thing. I'm sorry." His face flushed as he turned away from her. It was better this way. The shame was too great. He dared not admit to her his true intentions. No, better for her to think he was crazy and retain her precious innocence than to know what kind of creature he was. Yes, it was certainly better this way.

No footsteps followed him, no voice. He never turned back to see her expression. He didn't want to know. Better this way, better not to know. He hated himself for the person he had been. He was a different person now, that much was true. Leo Harr understood his own evil now, understood his own brokenness. Did that make him good? No, it just made him aware. Perhaps awareness was the first step on the path to righteousness. He chuckled. There was no righteousness for Leo Harr. Even salvation might not be in the cards for someone like him.

The pill bottle flashed before him; this time followed by an image of Connie's innocent face. What truly was the difference between Lucille lying to him about the pills and him lying to Connie about the painting? Lucille's lie seemed the lesser evil now. At least she was trying to help. Leo had only been trying to please himself, to satiate his own desires and hungers. Maybe Lucille wasn't the monster he had made her into, maybe he was the monster. Maybe Lucille was another victim of his. Maybe he had it all twisted in his mind.

Leo tossed the cigarette into the street and lit another, the last cigarette in the box. The darkness still lingered on the edges of his vision, but he no longer attributed it to some other dimension or faceless obsidian figures. No, that darkness was his, it always had been. It lived inside of him; it was a part of him; it had been all along. Then where had that light come from, those colors, that brilliant perfect triangle? It had to have come from somewhere else if it didn't come from inside of him, and he knew now that it couldn't have. No, he was much too full of darkness for that.

CHAPTER 20

THE LAST SUPPER

Leo scraped the Lo Mein onto his plate with chopsticks, one eye focused on Lucille who sat ever so properly across the table, and the other on his food. A pile of empty Chinese food containers littered the table, dripping sauce and grease across its surface. Lucille didn't seem to mind. Her head was down, her eyes focused on the food.

She devoured it all. So much food. How could someone so small eat so much? Did she always eat like this? Perhaps she was bulimic. It would make sense, and it wouldn't be out of character. A lot of women in Lucille's position were bulimic. Leo watched the Lo Mein slide out of the container as he pondered whether it mattered to him. No, he didn't really care, nor did he want to know. That was her business. He was happy to let her keep this secret.

A clock ticked in another room, the only constant source of noise that broke through the thick and pervasive silence. This house was a tomb, too silent and too stale. There were never any noises here, never any air movement. Just the same silence, the same ticking clock, the same stagnant air day in and day out.

Had this place always been like this? He racked his brain for memories of a time before, before all the madness, before the insanity. There were none. Everything started with the ringing phone and ended with the ticking clock and the smell of cheap Chinese food. There was nothing before, and there would be nothing after.

His eyes darted towards her purse, resting on an end table by the door. She had swapped the white purse with a black one to match the color of her dress. This purse, and dress, were even smaller than the last. Were the pills in there or were they still in the old one? The anger welled up inside of him again, that anger he had become all too comfortable with. Once upon a time he had thought of anger as the color red. Now it had a name, and its name was Lucille.

Leo brought a bit of the food to his lips, his eyes focused on the woman sitting across from him. She had already finished a box of Lo Mein and a box of sweet and sour chicken, now she was working on a box of beef and broccoli. How many calories was that? Why did he care?

He cared because she should have cared, because something about it was wrong, off, incorrect, and false. There was a Lucille he vaguely remembered who wouldn't so much as eat a donut, but here sat another Lucille, one who devoured thousands of empty calories without a second thought.

"So, why did you tell the doctors that you couldn't find the pills?" The words slipped out before he realized what had happened. He wanted them back, wanted to gather them up off the table and shove them back into his mouth, but it was too late. They were already sliding through her ear canal on the way to her brain.

She finished her bite of food, then placed her chopsticks on the plate and looked up, folding her hands beneath her chin as she smiled at him. He watched the mask slide into place as Aphrodite materialized before him.

"Mr. Russo and I looked everywhere. We just couldn't find them." Her voice was playful, too playful. Something in the way she enunciated certain sounds gave him goosebumps. He wanted to take her to bed right then and there. What had he asked her again? No, he couldn't let her do this. He had to be stronger than that.

"Did you check your purse?" His eyes never broke from hers. For a moment a darkness flashed across her face, a smoke-like shadow that coursed through her veins like lightning. It came and went so fast he wasn't certain he had seen it at all. Perhaps he was hallucinating.

"Why would I need to do that?" The smile never wavered, the grace never faltered, the beauty never faded, but a darkness settled in the space between them. A heavy, tangible thing, it swallowed the light, the sound, the space itself. He was closer to her now, and infinitely further away. Time crawled forward on its hands and knees, all the while sprinting as fast as it could away from some unseen enemy. Sweat pooled in his under-arms. His hands shook.

Leo considered dropping the line of questioning, finding a way to play it off, a way to return to his food and forget the entire thing ever happened. But what good would that do? It would just postpone the inevitable. Eventually the conversation would happen, and the more time that passed the angrier he would get and the longer she would have to construct an alibi. She was on to him now, if he let up and backed away she would win. He couldn't let her win.

"Don't play dumb Lucille," his voice was a whisper in that silence, the booming thunder of Zeus echoing through eternity. "I saw them. The pills. I saw them in your purse. Why did you lie to the doctors? Why did you lie to me? You could have helped me, you know! They could have told us what was in those damn things that nearly fucking killed me!" He realized he was screaming and snapped his mouth closed. The darkness closed in, the tiny infinite space between them squishing together, compressing into an even smaller space.

Lucille blinked once, then twice, then rose to her feet without saying a word. The clock ticked in the other room. *Tick, tick, tick.* Time went on forever, and in the next instant everything exploded in on itself in chaos and noise.

Lucille grabbed her chair and threw it across the room. It shattered as soon as it hit the wall, leaving massive scars in the wallpaper and drywall. The light fixture above the table rattled from the force.

"How dare you accuse me, Leo Harr!" She screamed, the shrill screeching of a harpy meeting the guttural base of a demon. "I paid for your rent! I paid for your medical bills! I've opened my door to you and this is how you repay me!? With accusations!" She slammed her fists against the table, then grabbed her plate and threw it at him. He ducked just in time as it whizzed by his head and struck the wall behind him, shattering into a thousand pieces and showering him with half-eaten beef and broccoli.

"What the fuck, Lucille! Calm down! Goddamn it, calm down!" Leo yelled as he rose from the chair, hands up in surrender.

Her eyes were wild, her face contorted in rage and anger. Gone was Aphrodite, gone was the motherly Demeter. They had been murdered, strangled, stabbed to death and in their place rose the Minotaur, raging and angry, more beast than human.

"I love you, Leo Harr! And this is how you repay my love!?" She snatched another plate and threw it at him. He ducked as it shattered above his head, small shards of the plate striking him on the shoulders and back of the neck.

"Calm the fuck down, Lucille!" He pleaded, inching towards the door. He needed to leave, he needed to get out of there and go as far from that place as he could.

"Calm down!? You're telling me to calm down!" Another plate exploded above his head. She was crazy, crazier than he was. That was the only explanation for any of this. Lucille Barett was a bat shit Looney-Toon, and Leo Harr–who himself wasn't very well strung together–had entwined himself with this absolute nut-job. Perfect. They complemented each other.

"Lucille! Stop it!" He stood up straight, lowering his hands, unwilling to cower any longer. Let her throw the plates, let her scream. This was insanity and he was over it. She stopped, and the mask returned, a placid and perfectly composed mask that settled in so fast that for a moment Leo questioned what had happened. Had he been the one throwing plates? Had she been angry at all?

"Oh Leo," her voice was full of desire, she wanted to make up. His heart raced at the idea. Gone was the thought of her throwing things and screaming, gone was the picture of her face contorted in rage. All that existed in his mind was the idea of taking her to bed. How glorious it would be. "I'm so sorry my love. I get carried away. Please forgive me."

She glided towards him, shoes crunching against the shattered plates. He took a step back, that bit of trepidation within him quickly dissipating as he watched her perfect curves flow towards him, her skin tight dress hinting at what hid beneath, tantalizing him, teasing him.

She reached out her hand and rubbed her fingers against his cheek. All he wanted was her, that was all he wanted in the entire world. Why had she been angry again? He had done something; it was definitely his fault. There was no other reason. Why couldn't he remember?

"I'll make it up to you, babe." The words echoed through time and space, rippling through the air and sending chills through his body. He locked his eyes onto hers, his mind swirling with the possibilities that they held. Oh, the horrible things he would do to her if he could just get her to bed. Or not. He could have her right there, right on the table.

No, this was madness.

"No, Lucille." He gently pushed her away as he stepped backwards towards the doorway. "What the fuck was that? That was fucking crazy."

He could see the rage flare behind her eyes but the mask didn't falter, not this time. She kept herself composed, but she was furious, furious at being rejected, furious that he hadn't just forgotten the entire thing. But Leo knew her games. She would tease him, tempt him, taunt him, and leave him with nothing, somehow slipping out of her own promises at the last minute without ever giving up a thing. It wouldn't work on him anymore.

"What do you mean, Leo?" She cocked her head to the side. Her voice was full of feigned innocence. He nearly laughed aloud.

"What do I mean? I mean the outburst, the fucking temper tantrum you just threw! You were trying to take my head off with plates!" He took another step back. He needed to get out of that room, he needed to get away from her.

"I don't know what you're talking about, Leo." Then she cried. Tears falling from her eyes as she lifted her hands to her face and collapsed in a heap on the floor. "Don't hurt me Leo! Please! Don't throw anything else, please don't!"

Leo's head reeled. He blinked several times, eyes scanning the mess of shattered plates, the gashes in the wall, the shards of broken chair, then falling back upon the huddled heap of Lucille as she wept on the floor. What was she talking about? He hadn't thrown anything. He played the memory back in his head, but this time it was different. Everything was different.

"Where are the fucking pills!" He yelled as he threw the chair against the wall, shattering it into a dozen pieces. "You fucking bitch tell me where you hid the fucking pills! I know you've been lying to me!" He threw a plate at her. She ducked just in time. Like a rabid animal, he snarled and snapped at her, hurling insults with poisonous intent.

Leo shook his head. No, that's not what had happened. Had it? Everything spun. The clock ticked from the other room.

Tick, tick, tick.

Lucille sobbed on the floor. No, it hadn't happened like that. He stepped back, eyes wild, hands extended as he braced himself against the wall. Why couldn't he remember? Why was everything such a blur? He leaned over and vomited, half-digested noodles and stomach acid splattering against his shoes. Wiping his mouth with his sleeve he took one last glance towards Lucille then fled, sprinting from the room as he lost himself in the winding hallways of her massive mansion.

CHAPTER 21

THE HOUSE

Leo stomped through the house, muttering to himself as he moved through hallway after hallway, meandering aimlessly. There were still blotches of grease and shards of plates on his clothes. How could he have been the one throwing the plates? He hadn't been angry at all, had he? She was crazier than he was. That was the only explanation.

The memory played out a hundred different ways. In one he was standing on the table, yelling about the end of the world while he poured the food over his head and laughed manically. In another, he cowered as a monster with the face of Lucille hunted him, sniffing him out so she could destroy him. The worst part was, each time he remembered the scene, he remembered it an entirely different way. The memory was fluid, ever changing, not static the way memories were supposed to be.

He slammed his hand against the wall as he rounded another corner. The house seemed to stretch on forever. Did they measure this thing in square feet or acres? It hadn't seemed so large from the outside, in fact, there was no possible way it could be this large, but it was, and Leo accepted it without complaint. Why bother arguing or trying to make sense of it? There was no sense anymore, or at least he had lost all of his.

The hallway breathed, stretching before him, pulling away from him like a rubber band. Doors appeared in the walls where they hadn't been before, light fixtures, end tables, carpets, but never windows. He had noticed that. This place never seemed to create new windows, only doors. He blinked, and the hallway was back where it had been, regular length, normal size. But how far had he walked? Further than the length of the hallway for certain, yet he was back at the start as if he hadn't moved.

Leo shook his head; an emotion grew inside him. It wasn't frustration; it wasn't curiosity, or even fear. No, this was rage in its most distilled and purified form. The fear of being trapped had given way to the frustration of not being able to escape, which had transformed into a red-hot fiery anger. There it was. He glimpsed it for the first time in so very long. The red was back, a bit, not a lot, and not just anger, red anger. He smiled and chuckled to himself. That red was a comfort, that insignificant amount of color was enough to keep him going. Maybe he could find the rest of the colors now that he had found one of them.

The end of the hallway led to another hallway, which led to another, but Leo paid it no mind. Better to put space between himself and Lucille, the more distance the better. Had he passed these rooms before? It was impossible to know. The doors all looked the same, the same white with ornate decorations and trimming. The kind of doors rich people have for no other reason than because they're rich. A door is a door is a door, but rich people always insist on making their doors special, even though they open and close the same way as everyone else's.

A sound echoed from behind him. His blood froze, and he quickened his pace. It was Lucille. He could hear her crying out for him. She was far away though, perhaps on the other side of the house. He moved even faster. He had to put more space between them. How far was the other side of the house? A mile? A minute? A fraction of a fraction of an inch? There was no concept of space here. She could be on him in a moment.

Rounding a corner, he grabbed a doorknob and pushed open the door, sliding into the unlit room and silently shutting the door behind him. She would never know which room he was in. There were so many of them. He waited in the darkness, listening for any sounds coming from the hallway. A smell burned his nostrils, a smell he remembered, but only as if from a dream. The smell of ozone or burning electronics.

His heart jumped. Perhaps there was a short in a circuit somewhere. It might cause a fire. He needed to fix it.

Leo flicked on the light-switch, blinking twice as his eyes re-acclimated to the light. He turned from the door and his heart stopped. A tightness wrapped around him, pressing against his chest, slowing his heartbeat, making him unable to breathe. He wanted to vomit; he wanted to fall to the floor and weep until there was nothing left, but he just stood there, frozen, staring towards the other side of the room at a plain red door.

It was *the* door. The one he had seen in the darkness, the one he had been told to close. It was here, inside Lucille's home. It stood slightly ajar, the blackness beyond so impenetrable that it seemed to ooze outward, swallowing the light, seeping into the floor, crawling along the walls.

He couldn't move. His mind raced. What was he supposed to do? Did Lucille always know about this door? Of course she did, this was her home, this was her door. His breaths came in spurts, faltering and jagged. Tears fell from his eyes and his mouth contorted in sorrow. Lucille, his precious Lucille had betrayed him, had always been betraying him, would always betray him.

Leo swallowed hard, forcing his feet to uproot from the wood floor. His hands shook, his legs wobbled. Through tear-filled eyes the door was merely a blob of red, the same shade and color as his own internal rage. Where had that color gone? The anger was no more. The red, that perfect, wonderful red, it had vanished. In its place was nothing, no color at all, a void of space in his heart where color should have been, where it once was.

This door, it was red, but it was nothing. It pulled the color from this place, bleaching the brown from the floor, stripping the gray from the walls, peeling the orange from the light until there was nothing but white, stark white, and that hideous, terrible red door.

The door moved closer, then jumped further away, glitching through time and space as he inched his way towards it. This door, it wasn't real, it couldn't be real. There was no way such a thing could exist. He watched it bleach the room, but the room remained the same color as before. He watched the blackness beyond reach outward with smoky, formless arms, casting shadows along the walls that never materialized. It was an anomaly, a thing of perfect and complete madness. A symbol of his own, perhaps, or the symbol of another's.

Leo reached with shaking hand towards the doorknob. A thousand voices screamed inside of him, screamed at him to die, die, die, to rip the electrical wires out of the wall and hang himself with them, to jump from the tallest building or blow his brains out with the biggest shotgun he could find. "Jackson Pollock the walls!" They screamed. "Bring the color back!"

His hand touched that door knob. An icy chill exploded up his arm. Colder than ice it was the cold of death itself, the cold of the void, of space, of the heat death of the universe. Time warped around him, he could feel it, see it bending itself into a Mobius strip and folding in on itself like a black hole. Today was yesterday, yesterday was never, and last week was a year from now. It made sense to him, but it hurt, god it hurt. That cold, that bitter cold screaming up his arm, eating away at him, peeling the pigment from his skin. He watched it all flake away, the pink, the brown. He watched his arm turn a solid white as the color bled out, sucked into the door, swallowed by the darkness.

Something reached out. Something dark, formless, something with a hand that was not a hand grabbed the other side of the doorknob and slammed the door shut. Leo jumped, falling to the floor as he crawled backwards on his hands and knees. The darkness was gone, the door was closed, but no, it wasn't, they could still open it again. The color returned to the room, to his arm, but not to his soul. No, in his soul he could still feel that icy chill of death's bitter touch.

"It's not polite to go through people's things," Lucille's voice called from behind him.

Leo gasped, flipping around to face her, his muscles tense and ready for a fight. What was she? Not Lucille, no, something else. One of them? Reality Boxes, yes, it had to be. It had to be a mask, a play, a ruse. He was so dumb, so foolish to fall for it. But as his eyes fell upon her perfect curves, those ideas of betrayal floated away, gone like smoke. She was so perfect, so beautiful. How could he not trust her?

"I…" Leo stammered, pushing himself to his feet.

She smiled, but it was a cruel smile, a smile of sick pleasure derived from his fear. She stepped into the room, hips swiveling, heels clicking against the floor.

"Oh, Leo," she chided, shaking her head and biting her lower lip.

Leo stepped backwards. What was she going to do to him? No, not 'she'. He needed to remember that this was not Lucille. It couldn't be. It had to be something else. Yes, the shadow, the darkness he had seen behind her skin. It made sense now. She was one of them. What had they done with the real Lucille?

"Lucille, or whoever you are. Leave me alone. I'll leave, I'll go. I won't come back. Just leave me alone." His voice was a whisper, a fearful whisper that barely escaped his lips.

He felt the red door closing in with every backward step. He was caught, fully and completely caught between that horrible red door and her. There was no escape.

"Leo, darling." She stopped, standing still, arms by her side. Her smile was no longer cruel. No, it was sensual, tempting, taunting. Her eyes had that look of desire that caused his mind to swirl with a thousand horrible thoughts. "I'm not going to hurt you. But you aren't going to leave."

With that, she reached behind her back and unzipped the dress, letting it fall to the floor around her feet. Leo's mind went blank as he stood there, staring at the full and untethered glory of her naked flesh. More perfect than he ever could have imagined, more perfect than any woman he had ever seen. She was perfection, all of it.

There was no other use for that word but to describe her. She was Aphrodite incarnate.

He forgot everything. He forgot the door, the colors, the darkness. He forgot fear, anger, betrayal. There was nothing but her. She stepped forward. His pulse quickened. This was it, the moment her body had been promising him for so long.

Stepping towards her, they embraced each other, and as two became one, the color and the light were all swallowed up in some hideous void, but Leo didn't care at all. Let it burn, let it die, let it disintegrate forever. This was a moment of perfection. And as they writhed upon the floor like serpents, a slight creak whispered from the hinges of that red door, and those tendrils of darkness crept in, swallowing the room, the color, and both of them, collapsing the moment into a single frame of dark and perfect silence.

CHAPTER 22

THE MONSTER

Leo awoke with a start, jolting up and gasping for breath as his swirling vision struggled to focus on the surrounding room. He couldn't remember where he was or how he'd gotten there, all he remembered was creeping darkness and the cold icy chill of complete and utter fear. His lips were cracked, dry like the rest of his mouth. He craved water.

His sight finally adjusted. He sat atop the crimson couch, facing some strange painting. Only a single light from out in the hall illuminated this room, but that faint orange glow was enough. The painting seemed familiar, but he couldn't remember why. A dark, formless figure on a rowboat amidst a tumultuous black sea. Where had he seen this before? He leaned in closer. Why did the person have no face? The waters were painted with such intricate strokes that the waves seemed nearly photo-realistic, but the person rowing the boat was just a blob of colors. He snickered and muttered something under his breath about how pretentious the piece was.

As his feet touched the floor, a feeling of wrongness washed over him. He hadn't laid down here. How had he gotten here? Holes existed where memories should have been. He stepped out into the foyer, past the small lamp, and stared up at the yawning ceiling. There should have been plenty of light to illuminate it, but the darkness swallowed it up. There was so much darkness here. Darkness so complete that it seemed impossible. Corners that should have been at least faintly illuminated were pure inky black. Shadows were deeper, longer, as if in those dark corners and black shadows the house itself ceased to exist. A chill ran up his spine. Why was it so cold? He couldn't see his breath, but he felt like he should have been able to.

He stepped into the kitchen; he needed water. Lights were on all over the room, but this room seemed even darker than the last. It was then that he noticed the colors. The house seemed washed out, bleached, like the pigments had bled out with age, leaving behind only faint memories of a vibrancy that had once existed. What on earth was going on and why did he feel like he had seen all of this before?

A clock ticked from somewhere nearby, not in the room, but in an adjacent room, loud enough to break the silence and echo through the empty space.

Tick, tick, tick.

Leo wondered what time it was. The question seemed important, though he couldn't remember why.

He grabbed a glass from the cabinet and filled it from the sink. Even the water was black. It looked like tar oozing from the faucet. He blinked the image away. No, it was just his sleepy mind playing tricks on him.

Tick, tick, tick.

The clock crept ever forward, unseen, invisible like time itself. Counting down, always counting down. Why did he always feel like clocks were counting down? The numbers went up, the hours increased, but they were always counting down To what? What happened when time ran out? Leo didn't want to know the answer.

He sipped the water. He swore it had been cold when it came from the sink, but it was tepid now and it tasted like metal. He didn't remember it tasting like that earlier, but then again, he didn't remember earlier very well at all. How had he even found his way into this house and this kitchen? It didn't belong to him; it wasn't his apartment. He swallowed the water down with a single gulp, forcing himself not to think about the horrendous taste. As the last bit slid down his throat, he realized it hadn't tasted like metal at all, no; it had been ice cold, refreshing, perfect. What on earth was wrong with him?

Turning back towards the sink, his eyes fell on a small black purse resting atop the counter. Had it been there before, or was he just now noticing it? A fragment of a memory slid into place, and anger followed. He and Lucille had gotten into a fight over the pills. That was it. She had hidden them from him. He needed them, didn't he? He did. But why? He couldn't remember but it didn't matter.

He scanned the halls and listened for intruders. Only the ticking clock broke the silence. Cautiously reaching towards the purse, he opened it and his breath caught in his throat. There they were. He knew them instantly. Those white oblong pills. They were all there. Not a single one was missing. His heart pounded in his chest as he removed the pill bottle, holding it in trembling hands as he examined it. Yes, these were the right ones, not round like the bad pills.

Lucille would try to take them away again. He had to hide them. But where? He didn't know this place, and he no longer had things of his own. He could try to keep them on his person, but how long would that ruse hold? There was only one way to make sure she didn't find them.

Leo popped the safety cap off and dumped the remaining pills into his mouth. How many was that? Thirty? Forty? He held them in his mouth and refilled the glass before swallowing them down, gagging as too many slid into his throat at once. His mouth was empty. It was done.

He smiled. She couldn't stop him. She couldn't keep him from the pills now. What had they been for, anyway? And why was he so certain they were important?

A phone rang, echoing through the house, rattling against the glass and tile, shouting out for anyone who would listen. Leo recognized that ring, he recognized it all too well. That was why he needed the pills, that was why they were so important. A faint image of a triangle flashed in his head, all grayscale with ragged edges.

Leo stepped towards the sound, dropping the pill bottle on the floor without a care. Let her find it. What could she do?

Ring, ring.

This time a large crash followed the sound, a crash from somewhere deeper in the house. Leo jumped. He had never heard that sound before. One foot in front of the other, he kept moving, crawling, inching his way towards the doorway. It was hard to tell where the sound was coming from; the ringing was all around him.

Ring, ring.

The ringing was distorted; it sounded as if the telephone was under water. Leo leaned against the counter, closing his eyes as he waited for the next ring. He had to let his ears guide him, that was the only way. Another crash exploded through the silence, closer now, followed by another, and another.

Ring, ring.

The sound was even more distorted this time. Something was wrong. Another crash echoed through the home, rattling the floor, shaking pictures off the wall.

"Where is it!" A voice screamed. It was Lucille's. No, not Lucille's. It had belonged to her once, but this was not Lucille. This was something else. The red door, yes, that red door was here. His heart raced; his legs threatened to buckle. What was he going to do? He had to answer the phone, but he couldn't tell where it was.

Ring, ring.

"Stop it, stop it!" Another series of crashes rattled the house. She was going through every single room looking for that phone. He couldn't let her find it. If she found it, what might happen? Leo drew himself up, standing straight as he forced the fear down.

"It's in the kitchen!" He yelled at the top of his lungs. Even his own voice seemed different, as if he was screaming into a heavy sheet.

The slamming stopped, and everything fell silent save for the clock in the other room ticking ever onward.

Tick, tick, tick.

Leo waited, fists clenched, jaw set. What would happen when she appeared? Would she devour him?

Darkness fell upon the room in the way a lantern illuminates a gloomy place. Creeping through the doorway it entered the kitchen and swallowed it. He watched it crawl along the floor and the walls, inching its way in, devouring the light and color as it crept forward. He knew the source of that darkness; he knew its face, and it had the face of an angel.

She appeared in the doorway, though the doorway no longer existed. Its form, its color, its shape, all swallowed up by her darkness. She looked like Lucille, but he knew better now. She stared at him; eyes filled with hate.

She didn't move. He stood his ground. He wouldn't let her win, not this time. The image of Lucille shimmered, and then shattered, falling away into a thousand little shards, all swallowed by that hideous darkness. Beneath was nothing, a black, formless, shapeless, malice. It had no face; it had no eyes; it had no body. It simply was, though it entirely was not. He could see it, but it was not there. Only his mind gave the thing position in a house that no longer existed.

The creature scanned the room, swallowing in darkness everything its eyes fell upon. Its gaze settled on the empty pill bottle cast aside so casually upon the floor. A cold wind swept through the air. Anger, hatred, disgust, each one of these things tangible in that cold and terrible wind that moved neither fabric nor dust, blowing like a hurricane but still as a tomb.

"What have you done?" The voice existed in the void where words should have been. The concepts of the words being removed from the world as they were uttered, leaving nothing but perfect silence in their wake.

Leo did not move. He did not reply.

The darkness wavered for a moment, that hideous presence staring into him. He felt his soul go supernova, inverting upon itself, folding inward, forming a black hole that threatened to consume him from the inside out.

"Where is it?" The silence spoke. It wanted the telephone. It would do anything to achieve that goal. In its words existed that desire, that need, that all-consuming hatred.

"It's gone now, it stopped ringing." Leo's voice hit the darkness and exploded, pieces ricocheting off the floor, the ceiling, and the cabinets, bouncing back at him in a nonsensical mess.

A terrible scream emerged from the creature, shrill and deep, high-pitched and sub-sonic. It shook the floors, the walls; it rattled Leo's very DNA, threatening to unravel him into a mass of worthless goo. The bald man had called these creatures the Unraveled. Leo now understood why. That was what they did. Unraveled realities, existences, everything until there was nothing left but that perfect void, that monstrous blackness, that hideous nothing.

Leo's eyes scanned for an escape. There was only one. A doorway on the far side of the room. He would have to make a break for it, but where would he go from there? The red door. That's all there was, that's what he had to do. To find the red door and close it. If he didn't, this creature would kill him. No, it wouldn't just kill him, it would do worse things to him than that.

The darkness shuddered and then jumped forward, swallowing the room.

"You!" It screamed out, but this time it was audible, and its voice was Lucille's.

Leo sprinted towards the doorway, but he hardly moved. His feet were stuck in mud. He was running underwater, though there was no water here. He ran as fast as he could, but the darkness came faster. With every step he took, the doorway pulled further and further away while that terrible darkness gained on him with incredible speed.

He cried out, screaming with all he had as he pushed forward. The darkness laughed in response. With every step he narrowly avoided those creeping clouds of shadow and his complete and utter obliteration. He closed his eyes. This was it, the end. Death, or worse; destruction and obliteration. Leo Harr would be no more. It would be as if he had never been. No one would remember him, because everything would be consumed in that blackness, every memory he touched, every second of time he had ever occupied, all of it wiped away in an instant.

Ice crept up his back, tickling his neck one moment then burning the next. The cold was fire, and the fire was the flame of hell itself. It was here; it was on him. He felt it breathing down his neck, heard it licking its lips as it prepared to devour its prey. Worse even, he could smell it, the smell of burning ozone. The smell of a frying microchip. Acrid and abrasive it scalded his nostrils as he inhaled, blistering his throat, melting his eyes from their sockets.

Tears fell as he struggled to hold in his mind one final memory, any memory, anything at all before he met his end. An image of an inverted triangle floated to the surface, and Leo watched as it dissolved, consumed by the black and the darkness, swallowed whole by the shadow.

CHAPTER 23

THE DOOR

R*ing, ring.*
The sound echoed around and inside of him. Without warning that cold disappeared, that feeling of horrible dread disintegrated, and Leo opened his eyes. Before him hung a painting of a man in a rowboat, the one he had seen before. He remembered now. This was his painting; he had made that. How long ago had that been? Years, months?

A terrible rumbling shook the floor beneath his feet. Leo knew what that was. It was the monster moving through the house, swallowing it, consuming it, unraveling it. He had to find the door. That's all there was. He had to end this.

Leo rose from the couch, moving towards the door, peaking out into the room beyond. He scanned the foyer, searching the growing darkness for an even darker darkness beneath. It could hide anywhere, in any shadow, anywhere light didn't touch. He had to be careful. There wouldn't be another chance.

Doing his best to remain silent, he tiptoed through the foyer, moving through doorway after doorway, sliding into unfamiliar rooms, scanning the shadows, moving with no proper direction towards what he hoped was that strange never-ending hallway. How had he gotten there before? He had been lost. There was no logic to it except that he had stumbled across it. Would he stumble across it again?

Ring, ring.

The rumbling shook the house, rattling lamps and glassware off of shelves, each one screaming as it shattered against the floor. He gave up sneaking. There was no point. Speed was his game. He had to beat this monster, had to outrun it, had to make it to his destination before it realized where he was. Could it smell him? Could it hear him? Perhaps it could feel him through the floor.

Every room gave way to another, each a slight variation on the last. Leo never stopped running. Room after room moved by him, the rumbling beneath his feet growing stronger with every step. The rooms continued, an impossibility that Leo tried to ignore. His breathing labored and lungs burning for air, he pressed forward. Where was he going? He had no idea, but it didn't matter. He had a feeling that he just needed to be lost, that finding the red door relied upon it.

Ring, ring.

As he entered the next room, he realized he was back at the start. His feet fell upon that crimson carpet, his eyes darting towards the red couch. He stopped, spinning around as he examined his painting hanging in the same place upon that wall. His mind struggled to understand what was happening. All that running, all those rooms, and he was right back where he had started. He yelled, a burning fire of anger and rage that exploded from his mouth like dragon's breath. The rumbling stopped.

Let it come. Destruction was inevitable. Let it be over with.

Ring, ring.

Gulping air into his lungs, he started running once more. Room after room melted behind him, but he paid them no mind, he simply ran as fast as his legs would take him. His chest heaved, his dry mouth begged for water, but he never slowed.

Room after room after room he ran. The rumbling never returned. The phone never rang. The clocks never ticked. Time was broken, he knew it, he felt it. Time, reality, it was all shattered into a million pieces, cast to the wind. He knew how to fix it, but he had to find that door.

Leo sprinted towards yet another doorway, his eyes showing him a similar room beyond that melted away into a total and complete blackness as he stepped through the threshold into a void of inky darkness. His feet rested on nothing; his body hung in the nether. Was he falling? He could have been and it would have made no difference. He had been here before, but it had been those strange pills. What brought him here now?

Fear coursed through his veins. Had the monster caught him? Was this the beginning of his destruction?

A red door appeared, far away, barely visible. Leo sprinted towards it, running through the nothing as his legs carried him closer and closer. There was no sound, no beating of his heart, no clicking of his shoes, no wheezing or labored breath. There was only silence. Perfect, deafening silence.

The door grew as he approached it, growing in size until it towered above him. He stood no taller than an ant, staring up at this horrible, monstrous thing. Then the door was gone. It didn't flicker; it didn't waver. It vanished.

"Hello Leo," Lucille's voice cut through the silence, falling into the surrounding darkness, not so much echoing as disintegrating.

Leo turned. The red door was there, back at a regular size, and before it stood Lucille. She smiled at him with that taunting, teasing smile as she stepped towards him, heels clicking impossibly against the darkness.

"You aren't Lucille," Leo whispered, his voice louder than a scream. He watched his words materialize into ribbons of color that fell away in pieces around him, swallowed by that hungry black.

Lucille laughed and nodded her head, "Of course I am silly. I always have been." She cocked her head to the side, eyes studying him. There was no hate behind those eyes, no, just the twinkling of desire. He pushed that terrible hunger away. She wouldn't get him this time, it wouldn't work. It couldn't. His eyes focused behind her on the red door. He had to reach it, he had to get to it.

"I'm certain you're curious how we got here. No doubt your memory isn't what it used to be," she chuckled. "We've been here since the party, when you in your drug filled stupor managed to crash through the Break and open the door. Thank you, by the way. Thank you for letting us in. We watched you, followed you. We watched that phone ring every night, and we knew one day they would come for you. We watched you answer the first call, and we knew what had to be done. She put up a fight, that one, oh she tried to keep us out, but she failed, like so many do.

"Remember the check? It listened to every word you two said. I thought I could manipulate you by just being her, but it wasn't working anymore. So, I gave you a little something, a treat, a subtle change. My error was in not destroying the original medication. You've taken them all, haven't you? It's a wonder your mind is still functioning."

Leo blinked; the memories crashed down upon him. All of it came back, every memory slamming into him like a tidal wave. He saw it all, the entire thing, the way she had manipulated him right into her grasp.

"No matter. We don't want you. We've never wanted you. We want them. They'll try to contact you again, and we'll find that phone, and you will help us. Don't be afraid. We won't destroy you until we're done with you. And maybe, if you're a good boy, we won't destroy you at all."

Leo clenched his fists. A slight hint of red flashed inside of him, a small red spark that grew into a flame. Suddenly the green and the blue, the yellow and the purple, the white and the orange were all there. Every color dancing in his mind, each a distinct emotion, a distinct feeling, a distinct thing he could not express in any other way but with color. All of them were there now. He felt the excitement, the beauty, the joy as they returned, but no, they needed to go, there was no room for them, he had no need for anything but the red. He let the red swallow them; he let them die.

"No," he stated, voice howling in the dark, the words falling from his lips in red flakes that floated towards the door, "no more."

Lucille laughed aloud, a musical sound that sent chills up his spine.

"Oh Leo. It's over, dear. We've won. We've always won. You were never fit to save anyone, to change anything."

The red inverted, folding in on itself, consuming itself. They were just words; he tried to tell himself that, but those words destroyed him, unraveled him, broke him. He fought it, but it was too much. He felt himself giving up, falling down, collapsing. And then, a hint of an idea flashed just beyond the black, just behind the swirling red and the sorrow. A final attempt, a last-ditch effort.

"You're right," he muttered, stepping forward.

A smile crept across Lucille's face. "Of course, I am Leo. Now. Will you help us and save yourself?"

Leo's footsteps rattled in the darkness as he moved towards her. He hated her, hated her for being beautiful, hated her for everything she had done to him. He hated her more than anything he had ever hated in his life.

"If I can have you again." His words caused her smile to grow even larger. A sensuality fell across her face, a desire growing behind her eyes as that mask slid into place.

"Of course, Leo, whatever makes it hurt less."

With that, she unzipped her dress. Leo didn't look, his eyes focused instead on the red door. He stepped forward, extending his arm as he grasped her naked body in a tight embrace. He drew her head close to his, their lips connecting. Her eyes closed, but his eyes never left that door.

With one swift motion, Leo spun her around and grabbed the icy doorknob. He pulled the door wide open. An even darker darkness reached out, tendrils wrapping around him, silent screams of lost souls calling to him from beyond. He didn't care. Let it destroy him. He would fix what he had broken.

"No!" She screamed, but it was too late. Leo grabbed her arm tight and pulled her forward. She staggered, crashing into him with all her weight. His hand still on the doorknob, they fell, and the darkness swallowed them as the door slammed shut.

Leo watched her disintegrate, unraveling, unspooling like a ball of yarn. Her body, her soul, her entire being scattered like embers in the darkness. He felt a rumble as the void consumed every piece, every scrap, every shred. This darkness was alive, and it was hungry. A cloud of cold nothing wrapped around his neck, pulling him down into the dark. He didn't struggle; he didn't scream. Instead, he closed his eyes and pictured himself upon that rowboat, rowing through the glassy black waters.

Leo smiled. He had won. It was over. And as he smiled, he felt the icy filaments dig into him, burying themselves in every strand of his DNA as it tore him apart. Then he saw it, rising from the darkness, breaking free of the last fragment of Lucille's form. That faceless obsidian monster growled at him and then swallowed him whole.

CHAPTER 24

THE END

"How long has he been like this?" Officer Jessop asked between sips of coffee, eyes peering through swirling steam into the interrogation room beyond. Someone needed to clean that thing. It looked like it hadn't been wiped down in a decade. The once-white tile floor was stained brown with grime and the gray paint was peeling off the walls, revealing the concrete. How did a single-purpose room get so filthy?

"Since we picked him up." Voice like gravel, Officer Benson leaned back against the desk. This was technically his case; Jessop was just there to assist. Something about the suspect being in a near comatose state, unresponsive to any questioning, unwilling to speak a word, possibly unable. Those types were Jessop's specialty. He excelled with the mentally handicapped. His father always joked that it was because they were kindred spirits, something, something, Jessop was autistic. Very funny dad. No, it was just about finding some kind of common ground. Most officers treated everyone like a criminal. It didn't work very well with normal people, much less people with below-average faculties.

Jessop sipped his coffee, studying the man hunched over in the metal chair, eyes staring at the only light bulb in the room. He wasn't handcuffed. He hadn't put up any kind of resistance, so the officers hadn't thought it necessary. Jessop couldn't help but chuckle to himself. They bolted the chair to the floor, but allowed a murder suspect to remain free to do as he pleased. Something about it seemed ridiculous.

The suspect was a white male, early to mid-thirties, probably would have been fairly handsome if he didn't look like a complete wreck. Story was that he was some well-known local artist. Jessop couldn't see how. The man was a vegetable, practically drooling on himself as he sat there. Had he even blinked since they booked him?

"Run through the details again, I want them fresh before I go in there." Jessop wasn't in charge here, but he spoke like he was. Hell, it didn't matter who was in charge. They had a job to do. They had to get this guy to confess, or if not, then figure out who killed that woman and bring them in.

"Not much to tell really," Benson started, "found him wandering around outside the house. The neighbors called it in. They heard a bunch of noise coming from the Barett place. They thought it was a wild animal at first, then they saw him poking around, yelling and screaming about triangles and doors. They were afraid he would hurt someone. Officers arrived on scene. Sure enough, he was raving about some door and a telephone like a goddamned loon, right there on Miss Barett's front porch. Well, the door was wide open and there was no sign of Miss Barett, so officers searched the premises. That's when they found the body. Coroner is still working on a cause of death, but the body had been there for a while. Weeks, probably. Thing was in an awful state of decomposition. Only leads we have are this psychopath, but honestly we can't even tie him to the murder, not really. I mean, we're gonna charge him, but there's no evidence. That's why you're here."

Jessop nodded; eyes still focused on the suspect in the other room.

"Did you see the body?" Benson asked.

Jessop shook his head. He hadn't wanted to. Things like that clouded your opinion of a person, enraged you, made you question people differently. He always waited until after questioning, if he looked at all.

"Had to have been at least a month of decomposition. Jessop, that thing was some kind of rotten."

"Was there any DNA on the suspect?"

Benson shook his head and then chuckled uncomfortably. "Nothing at all."

"It doesn't make any sense," Jessup muttered under his breath.

"No, it sure doesn't."

Jessop took a deep breath. It was time to ask Mr. Harr what he knew. Time to break through and get some answers. He stepped through the door into the hall. The sound of a busy police station echoed against the tile and concrete, bouncing off the fluorescent bulbs before heading back the way it came. Jessop readied himself, taking a deep breath before entering the interrogation room.

A smell filled his nostrils as soon as he entered. Ozone? Electrical Fire? It was gone as quick as it came. Maybe a bug had committed suicide on one of the lightbulbs. Jessop moved towards the table and took his seat across from Mr. Harr, folding his arms and crossing his foot over his knee. Something about this man made Jessop uncomfortable, and it wasn't just the fact that he might be a murderer. Jessop had dealt with plenty of those.

"Mr. Harr, my name is Officer Jessop. How are you doing today?" He softened the edges of his voice. It was important to talk to people in these states at their level, not like children, but not harsh, or judgmental, or condescending. He needed to connect with Mr. Harr, not scare him.

After several moments of silence, Jessop started again.

"Mr. Harr, I'm here to help you. I just have a few questions if that's okay. Or, if you'd like, we can talk about something else."

Mr. Harr replied with silence, his eyes focused up on the lights above. He didn't blink, even though it was obvious his eyes were burning. He had to be in considerable pain. Bloodshot and dry they stared into that light unwavering. For a moment Jessop wondered if the man was even still breathing. Only the faintest noise confirmed the suspect was, in fact, still alive.

"Mr. Harr," Jessop unfolded his arms and leaned forward against the metal table, "I need to know your side of the story here. I have to know what happened."

Almost imperceptibly at first, Mr. Harr's eyes moved from the light, down towards Jessop, finally focusing directly on the officer's face. Mr. Harr blinked once, then twice. His mouth curling into a smile, but that smile quickly inverted into a look of terror.

"It's done," he whispered; his voice barely audible.

Jessop leaned in further. "It's done? What's done, Mr. Harr?"

"It's closed."

"Closed?"

Mr. Harr nodded, his mouth moving silently as if he was speaking inaudible words. Jessop noticed the man's hands were trembling.

"Mr. Harr, what happened to Miss Barett?"

The suspect shook his head, a look of terror flashing behind his eyes. "Not Lucille. Not anymore."

Jessop paused. What did he mean by that?

"Mr. Harr, listen to me. Now, I know this is difficult, but we have a dead woman on our hands, and the only person who can help us find her killer is you. I need to know what you know; I need to understand what you understand."

Mr. Harr blinked again and then turned his eyes back towards the light. The look of terror flipped into a smile that crept back across his face, growing and growing until it revealed his teeth and gums. A tear rolled down his cheek.

"You can't understand because you've never seen it. I've seen it." The man sat up straight, his entire face falling back to normal as if he had just woken up inside his own body. His eyes fell upon Officer Jessop. Mr. Harr breathed deep, eyes widening, tears falling from his cheeks as a look of pure ecstasy washed over him.

"I never thought I would see it again, but..."

The suspect paused, and then collapsed, sliding out of the chair and slamming into the tile floor. Jessop jumped out of his chair and rushed to the man's side. He called out for help as he cradled the disheveled man's head in his arms. Mr. Harr was still breathing, though barely. The breaths came in quick bursts, ragged and shallow. His eyes rolled back in his head, though his face was perfectly at peace, almost glowing with calm and warmth. It wasn't a seizure, no this was something else, a heart attack maybe? No, that didn't fit the symptoms either.

Mr. Harr's muscles went rigid as steel and then completely relaxed, and with the last bit of breath in his lungs he uttered his final words.

"I see it now. And it's beautiful."